SHE COULD FIGHT HIS BRUTALITY,
BUT SHE HAD NO STRENGTH AGAINST THIS
. . . THIS SWEETNESS . . .

Her heart began to beat against her rib cage like the wings of a frightened butterfly. He grazed his beard across her palm, then closed her hand over his mouth and bit softly. Her legs turned to water and nearly buckled. Only Heath could affect her like this.

"I want to make love to you on these cold lonely nights," he whispered thickly, his eyes turning dark and sleepy with desire. She was drowning. A woman's sweet poignant need washed over her, wrenching the breath from her lungs and paralyzing her thought processes. In another moment he would take her in his arms and she would be lost . . .

A CANDLELIGHT ECSTASY ROMANCE ®

TENDER TORMENT

Harper McBride

A CANDLELIGHT ECSTASY ROMANCE ®

Published by
Dell Publishing Co., Inc.
1 Dag Hammarskjold Plaza
New York, New York 10017

Dell ® TM 681510, Dell Publishing Co., Inc.

Candlelight Ecstasy Romance®, 1,203,540, is a registered
trademark of Dell Publishing Co., Inc.,
New York, New York.

ISBN: 0-440-18584-X

Printed in the United States of America
First printing—September 1983

To Our Readers:

We have been delighted with your enthusiastic response to Candlelight Ecstasy Romances®, and we thank you for the interest you have shown in this exciting series.

In the upcoming months we will continue to present the distinctive sensuous love stories you have come to expect only from Ecstasy. We look forward to bringing you many more books from your favorite authors and also the very finest work from new authors of contemporary romantic fiction.

As always, we are striving to present the unique, absorbing love stories that you enjoy most—books that are more than ordinary romance.

Your suggestions and comments are always welcome. Please write to us at the address below.

Sincerely,

The Editors
Candlelight Romances
1 Dag Hammarskjold Plaza
New York, New York 10017

CHAPTER ONE

Shelby stared with frightened tenseness at the two men who were her abductors. They did not look like criminal types—one being a clean-cut, blond, boyish-looking man; the other a tall, elderly man with chiseled features.

She collapsed on her sofa as her legs suddenly lost the power to keep her upright. A wave of panic washed over her, and she struggled to rise above its suffocating force. It had been a terrible shock to have been met by these two strangers upon arriving home from work today. They had taken possession of her tiny apartment even to the extent of packing her suitcases for her. The blond one had informed her to her astonished face that they had broken in and intended to take her captive, adding with a lopsided, charming smile that he hoped she would not be difficult about it.

A blanket of tense silence enveloped the room as they waited for her reaction. She forced a shaky laugh through even, clenched teeth and tried to be casual.

"Why kidnap *me?*" she challenged. "My father might be state representative of Florida, but believe me he wouldn't give you a dime's worth for me. Why, I haven't even seen him for three years, except in the newspapers and on television occasionally. He has forgotten I exist."

"Your father doesn't interest us," the fair one informed her with a winning smile.

Shelby couldn't help noticing how nice this man looked. But then, she had learned from TV thrillers that the easygoing, nice-looking ones were usually the cruelest.

Oh, this can't be happening, she cried inwardly. She cast a frightened sky-blue glance about her living room as if expecting suddenly to discover a magic open sesame of escape. I live a quiet life. I don't bother anybody. I'm just an ordinary working woman who enjoys a normal social life and is reasonably content in her little one-bedroom apartment. She lifted panic-stricken eyes to the ceiling as if pleading with someone beyond that spackled solid expanse. Oh, what have I ever done to deserve this!

Guilt stabbed her like a flaming rapier. She *had* done something long ago for which she was deeply ashamed. Perhaps this was just retribution for that terrible deed. Even though it had happened seven years ago and could have nothing whatever to do with her present predicament, perhaps judgment for that horrible mistake was finally about to descend on her head. After all, wasn't it said that sooner or later one had to pay for one's sins?

She made a visible effort to pull herself together. "Since Father won't be an easy touch for the ransom, I suppose you intend to demand it of my brother-in-law. Every cent of his money is tied up in his citrus grove. So you see, I'm a bad bargain." Convulsively swallowing the lump of horror in her throat, she added bravely, "Go off and abduct someone more promising."

"We're not after money, Miss Constantine," the clean-shaven young man stated firmly.

"Then what do you want?" she queried in bewilderment.

"Just you." He gave her a sickly smile, as if the whole situation was suddenly as distasteful to him as it was to her.

She looked at him incredulously, then at the immobile old man whose face seemed to be carved out of ancient redwood. Finally, at long last, she opened her mouth to scream her lungs out.

But the sound died in her throat as a tough, weather-beaten hand closed over her mouth, shoving her back into the couch pillows. The old man gave her a dark, stony look, his cold eyes glittering unpityingly. She saw ruthless determination etched in his sharp features and knew that here was real danger.

"You have two choices, Miss Constantine," he said with deadly intensity. "You can come with us quietly and we will not harm a hair on your pretty head. Or . . ." He paused for effect, and she saw the blade of a knife flash suddenly under her chin. "Have you seen the Indian and his various methods of persuasion on the late-night television movies, Miss Constantine?" he asked mildly. Her eyes widened to two blue lakes of stark fear. "I am an Indian." His voice was chillingly quiet. The tip of the knife flicked against the alabaster skin of her throat.

The other kidnapper gave an astonished gasp. She dared not move, dared not swallow.

"I will not give you gory details," he went on with cool seriousness. "I'll leave that to your imagination." The point of the blade raked harmlessly but threateningly down the curve of her throat.

"For God's sake, Joe Sam! Take it easy," the other man burst out.

The Indian's glittering, intelligent eyes never left her face. Her smooth white pallor contrasted startlingly with his wrinkled sun-baked roughness. He scrutinized every expression fleeting across her clearly readable face—fear, helplessness, then finally courage.

A barely perceptible smile lifted one corner of his mouth. "You will come peaceably then?" It was a statement of fact rather than a question.

Her lips mouthed "Yes," for a nod would have sent the knife a half inch into her flawless, creamy throat.

The young one let out a deep sigh of relief. "You won't regret your decision, Miss Constantine," he gushed thankfully. "It's not our intention to harm you. We're not criminals. We're just . . ."

"Quiet, Aaron," the Indian cut in. "Grab her bags and let's go."

"Yes, of course," he acquiesced.

A tough, bronzed hand steered her out the door and down the stairs of the apartment building to a parked car. Aaron put her bags in the trunk. Joe Sam motioned her to get in the front seat and then took a place beside her. Apparently the blond, good-looking Aaron was going to drive.

At once her landlady, infamous for her curiosity in all comings and goings of the tenants in Palm Haven Apartment Building, opened the door of her ground-floor quarters to make a nosy, meandering foray for information.

"Going on vacation, Shelby?" she asked, approaching the car. "I couldn't help noticing the luggage."

Shelby filled her lungs to scream for help, but a touch of steel against her rib cage quashed this impulse immediately.

"Yes," Aaron answered blandly, taking his place behind the wheel. "Isn't it wonderful? Miss . . . er . . . Shelby is going to the mountains for an extended vacation."

Mrs. Eversole fanned her face with a bony hand. "Oh, so nice in the mountains this time of year. You're lucky to be escaping this heat." She ducked to address Shelby and favor her with a grin. "I've never known the end of September to be so uncommonly hot in Florida. If this keeps up we'll have no winter at all. I do hope you cleaned out the refrigerator, dear." Shelby's heart sank; the garrulous woman was not the least bit suspicious that foul play was being conducted right under her hawkish nose. "How long will you be gone?" she asked cheerily. "Where will you be staying? Should I forward your mail, or will your sister be picking it up?"

"Yes," Aaron answered desperately, as if he hadn't thought of this detail. "Her sister will pick up her mail." He focused grimly on the ignition and turned the key.

Mrs. Eversole was not to be put off so easily. She stepped forward in friendly inquisitiveness. "I don't believe I've had the pleasure of meeting you," she said, openly admiring Aaron's clean good looks. "I don't seem to remember you among Shelby's many admirers."

"Oh, we haven't known each other long," he responded glibly. "But I'm already very fond of Shelby. Quite a woman." He concluded this abominable lie by patting her knee affectionately, at which she recoiled in a horror of disgust. Ignoring this telling reaction, he added, "I just can't wait to show her to my folks."

Mrs. Eversole's sharp nose twitched as she fancied the delicious scent of romance in the air. "Oh, how wonderful! And your folks live in the mountains. Appalachian or Rockies?"

"Let's get out of here," the Indian growled under his breath.

Aaron eased the car slowly away from the curb. "Rock-ies."

"But when will you be bringing her back?" the scrawny woman pursued relentlessly.

Aaron cast her a sly glance meant to convey romantic intrigue. "Maybe never."

Completely taken in, Mrs. Eversole laughed and waved gaily. "Have a good time."

Shelby dropped her head and gave a slow, desperate sob. What did these men want with her? Would she ever return to her comfortable little apartment? What would Mr. Tate say when she didn't show up for work Monday?

Questions lay in her mind like a tangled skein. Who were these awful men? Did they want to kill her? If so, they could have already done it within the quiet confines of her living room. If they were not after money and not pathological maniacs, then what were they? Just your everyday, run-of-the-mill friendly kidnappers? It didn't make sense. None of this made any sense at all.

She stole a glance at the Indian's immobile profile, no-ble, like the imprint on a silver nickel, then at the fair Aaron, who for all his easy chatter seemed vastly uncomfortable, as evidenced by the great drops of perspiration trickling beneath the neck of his expensive Hawaiian-print shirt.

Aaron drove through the highways of Orlando to a small privately owned airport. After parking the car, he turned to his stone-faced accomplice. "I'll take care of the luggage and make arrangements for the rental car to be picked up while you get her on the plane."

Joe Sam circled Shelby's wrist with a band of iron and tugged her none too gently from the car.

"You're hurting me, you old bastard!" Some of Shelby's

12

fear had given way to anger and indignation. She was a woman known for her temper, which often blazed up impulsively like a blue-hot flame, and a distinctive tendency toward extreme stubbornness.

He tightened his grip, remarking tonelessly, "You have a warrior's spirit. Unusual in a female. Most women would have fainted or gone into hysterics by now."

"Where would that get me?" she spat, rosy anger staining her cheeks. "I intend to get out of this mess. Alive!"

He pulled her across the airfield toward a Twin Comanche four-passenger aircraft painted bright yellow. Glancing at her delicate profile, the old man sensed that beneath the fresh innocent skin, the bewitching azure eyes, and the long curtain of lush hair now gleaming blue-black in the sun was a woman of deep strength and courage. And no matter what else he had been told about her, he had to admire that.

"You have a fierce sense of self-preservation, Miss Constantine."

His calm, expressionless face goaded her into speaking rashly. "Just don't leave your knife lying around, Mr. Joe Sam, or whatever your name is, because you might find it stuck neatly between your shoulder blades."

The barest hint of a smile again touched his old wizened mouth. "You would make a good squaw," he grunted, "except for the blue eyes. I will call you Summer Sky." He intoned this as if bestowing a great honor.

"Thanks," she sneered, her voice wobbling at the edges.

He opened the small door of the aircraft and motioned her in.

"I will not ride in this ridiculous tin can." She dug her heels into the tarmac and refused to budge. "I have a

13

phobia of flying in a small craft. You'll just have to take me by car."

"That's impossible, Summer Sky," he grunted. Without further argument he flung her over his shoulder and climbed into the Comanche, tossing her onto one of the seats like a sack of potatoes.

Briefly and silently she acknowledged the physical strength of this amazing old man. Then she lashed out to struggle and claw. He deftly caught her hands and held them fast.

"Hand me that rope," he ordered Aaron as the young man came through the door, throwing in her luggage.

Aaron obeyed reluctantly. "Do we have to tie her up?"

Joe Sam pulled her arms in back of the seat and knotted the rope firmly around them. "She's more angry than frightened now," he remarked wisely. "Never trust an angry squaw or a trapped one."

Aaron looked bedraggled in his colorful sweat-stained shirt. Weariness and fear passed across his handsome face fleetingly. He gazed into Shelby's wide azure eyes with something like pity. "The lengths to which one will go for a friend," he muttered enigmatically.

They both stood back to regard her dispassionately, as if she were an exotic pinned butterfly. "She's the key," the Indian intoned lowly. "We're doing the right thing."

Aaron ran his fingers through his fair hair and sighed deeply. "I hope to God you're right. We've risked going to prison for pulling this stunt."

"I would rather go to prison than see White Brave go on as he is," said Joe Sam.

"Well, at least we would have a top-notch defense lawyer." Aaron laughed mirthlessly.

Shelby had been listening to this interchange intently.

"Who the devil is White Brave?" she blazed. "Another cutthroat criminal, I suppose."

Joe Sam ignored her and took the pilot's seat, followed closely by Aaron, who sat down beside him. "Get some rest," the old man urged her. "We've a long trip ahead."

Her stomach lurched crazily as the yellow Comanche roared into the sky like some gigantic gleaming canary. She had only ridden on an airplane a few times, and never on one this small. There was something decidedly unnerving about trusting oneself to the bowels of a metal man-made machine with only the thin substance of sky above and below as a cushion. But this eccentric fear was quite overshadowed by the very real danger of her present victimized state.

These men had not harmed her, yet surely there was some purpose behind this abduction. No matter what they said, it had to be money. Obviously they were taking her to a hideout somewhere. Then they would probably get in touch with her father and demand a sizable ransom.

She gave a small malicious laugh as she imagined the look on her father's face as he discovered her kidnapping. They had about as much chance of getting money out of him as an ice skater had of enjoying a holiday in Hades. Oh yes, he had plenty of money. But he wouldn't waste it to rescue her; he would merely dutifully turn the whole affair over to the authorities and go on with his life. He had in effect disowned her seven years ago, after that hideous court trial. And since his marriage to a prominent news correspondent four years ago, he had barely spoken to her, acknowledging her existence only at Christmas time, when some totally unsuitable gift arrived by mail with curt good wishes scrawled on a card in his wife's hand.

Leaning as far forward as she could in her trussed position, she peered out the window of the aircraft, the yellow wing of which had caught the gleam of the late afternoon dying sun. Clouds floated by like gossamer veils, and she became fascinated with the scene below.

Viewing it put one in a position of detachment where the earth seemed a faraway place. But instead of the world seeming small with its miniature palm trees, neatly spaced grove land, and lakes which looked like puddles, it was Shelby who felt infinitesimal and quite, quite powerless.

She eased back in the seat as staying in the forward position put too much strain on her arms. She regarded the two men thoughtfully, not as frightened of them now as she had been at first. Aaron had the look of the junior executive about him. He reminded her a lot of Mr. Tate, her boss, even though there was at least twenty-five years' difference in the two versions.

Lord! she exclaimed silently. What would all this do to her job? What would Mr. Tate think when she didn't show up for work Monday morning? His young niece had been vying for Shelby's enviable position for weeks. At this rate, it looked as if she had a good chance of becoming Mr. Tate's private secretary after all.

Shelby twisted the restraining rope around her wrists. She hated inactivity. The constant drone of the airplane motor and the bland blue sky were not her idea of audio and visual entertainment. She chafed under her enforced solitude, despising any kind of solitude whatsoever. Her sister had once stated that this idiosyncrasy was another side effect of the trial. Shelby had admitted ruefully that she was probably right: being alone with her guilt-drenched memories was too painful to be endured.

At home on the few evenings she was not with friends,

she filled her hours in the apartment by cleaning, sewing, or washing clothes. The television was always on for company. She liked its noisy chatter, and although seldom really sitting down to watch, she flipped it on the moment she hit the door as a matter of habit.

Her sister, Luann, said she was neurotic. No normal person required diversion every waking moment of the day. Luann had advised her to forget the trial and Heath Tanner, the man she had ruined. A person could not go on feeling guilt and remorse forever. Shelby had remained quiet, knowing she could never forget Heath or what her willful and foolish actions had done to him.

Poor Luann. What would she think when Shelby didn't show up on Sunday? Shelby hadn't missed a Sunday dinner with her sister's family since moving out four years ago. Suddenly she experienced a flash of hope. Of course! Luann would know something was wrong. Perhaps Mr. Tate would too, since Shelby had never missed a day's work without calling in first. They would contact the police. The police would find her.

The small plane was soaring through black sky now. She had no idea how far away she was from home. She strained forward and peered out the window again. Rows of lights greeted her from below. The plane descended, then touched down for a soft landing.

"Beautifully done," Aaron praised the old Indian.

As they taxied to a smooth stop, Aaron took off his headgear and walked back to Shelby. "Time for a pit stop, Miss Constantine. We'll refuel here before going on. This is a small airport, but there are vending machines in the office. I'll get you coffee and a sandwich." He smiled. Again, it was uncanny how much he reminded her of Mr. Tate.

Joe Sam untied her and she rubbed her wrists gingerly. "If you won't try to run away, I'll escort you to the restroom so you can freshen up," he offered without inflection.

"You're a prince," she said, venomously sarcastic.

He stationed himself outside as she walked in and locked the door. Once inside, she noticed a narrow window high above the lavatory. A feeble plan of escape formed in her mind. She could climb up on the lavatory, shimmy out the window, drop noiselessly to the ground, and scuttle off quietly into the night. The arrogant old Indian could wait a patient eternity for her return to his evil clutches.

She smiled, threw cold water on her face and wrists, hiked her smartly tailored skirt above her knees, and climbed up on the sink. With suppressed grunts and groans she thrust herself head first through the window, shredding her sheer stocking on the inside wall in the process. Turning so that she was sitting in the narrow opening with her shapely derriere in precarious balance, she firmly grasped the window ledge and tucked her legs under her.

Now what was she going to do, she wondered, wobbling shakily on her knees. Gritting her teeth, she allowed her body to slide abrasively down the outside wall. Oh no. She hung there momentarily, realizing too late that the drop to the ground was at least three feet. She was sure to break an ankle when she landed in her slender, fashionable pumps.

Oh well, there was nothing left to do. Clenching her eyes tight, she let go, scraping her arms and ripping her silk blouse while sliding painfully to the ground. Her heels stabbed into gravel and she fell in a clumsy heap, breaking no bones thankfully.

Upon opening her eyes, her first view was the khaki-clad pant legs of the Indian. Her gaze traveled upward to his frozen face.

"Now see, you've torn your clothes and scraped yourself up." His voice was devoid of expression.

"Oh! You were watching the whole time," she cried wrathfully.

He picked her up by the arms. "Come along. Coffee and food will make you feel better. You can't escape. Face it."

"You can't blame me for trying!"

"No," he responded agreeably.

"Oh, please tell me what you want with me." She bit back tears of frustration and fear. "I don't understand any of this."

"White Brave will explain," he answered shortly while leading her up the stairs of the plane and depositing her firmly in her seat. "It's not my place."

"You dirty old . . ." Her efforts at escape being ineffectual, she had resorted helplessly to invective. "What's in this for you? A lot of money, I suppose."

"No money."

"What then?"

"The happiness of one I love," he answered without emotion or expression.

"Oh, that makes a lot of sense," she raved. "A helluva lot of sense."

"What happened to her?" Aaron asked, boarding the plane and eyeing her torn clothes and raked arms.

"She tried to escape," Joe Sam answered mildly while taking a sandwich out of its paper.

"Gutsy, isn't she?" Aaron remarked. "Here," he said,

shoving a sandwich toward her. "Eat something and drink your coffee. I'll doctor those scrapes afterward."

"You won't touch me," she warned through gritted teeth.

"Have it your way." He shrugged.

It seemed that this Aaron was a man who would go out of his way to avoid trouble. So why was he a kidnapper? Why would this apparently gentle and innocuous man want to abduct her? Her mind drew a fearful blank. She sniffed a little and sipped her coffee. Eating anything was out of the question, but the warm coffee soothed her.

Joe Sam got out the first aid kit and pinned down her unwilling arms, smearing the scratches with a generous amount of iodine. "I won't tie you up again."

"How considerate," she retorted, her sarcasm once again in full swing. "Someone should award you the Nobel Peace Prize."

"Can you pilot an aircraft, Miss Constantine?" he asked offhandedly.

"Of course not!"

"Then don't try something foolish like creeping up to attack us from behind once we are in the air. Without pilots this plane would plummet to a very sudden and definite stop." He closed the first aid kit with a click. "We'll be there in a couple of hours. Try to sleep."

They took their positions and soon the craft was again airborne. She turned in her seat, watched little lights race by below, and soon the only thing in view was an unfathomable blackness. She had never felt so alone in her life.

She comforted herself by imagining her rescue, closing her eyes, seeing these two unusual characters behind bars. But it was not these men she saw in prison but a man from her past, his handsome face strong and haggard and tormented, his velvet black eyes glittering with hatred. She tried to erase his face from her mind, but her tortured brain persisted in its remembering and held her captive more than these two criminals ever could.

There was the courtroom walled by dark wood paneling, enclosing a sea of curious faces. There was the shrewd prosecuting attorney barking questions at her—questions he and her father had previously told her to answer yes to. And she had. That was the awful part: she had. Her ambitious, politically minded father had used a method worse than physical punishment to exact her cooperation —emotional blackmail. And torn to pieces between loyalty and truth, love for family and love for a man, she had sent Heath Tanner, her first and only true love, to prison.

She would never forget those questions—that horrible twisting of the truth, that insidious mockery of justice.

"So you met the defendant, Mr. Tanner, at the construction sight where he worked, Miss Constantine?"

"Yes." The tremulous answer came from a demure schoolgirl dressed in a loose sailor blouse and a dark blue skirt that hid her womanly curves. Her long hair was tied back neatly with a white satin ribbon. Every detail of her appearance had been staged by her father and the prosecuting attorney, his friend, to effect innocence.

"Mr. Tanner noticed you going by every afternoon on your way home from school and struck up a friendship. Isn't that right?" he pursued.

"Yes," she stumbled. This wasn't exactly the truth. No, not at all.

"Eventually Mr. Tanner persuaded you to go out with him . . . alone . . . at night?" The question was deliberately loaded with innuendo.

"Yes." She cried inside. Oh, if I could only explain!

"So!" He turned dramatically to face the jury. "A twenty-four-year-old man of experience asks a mere seventeen-year-old schoolgirl for a date." He raised his brows significantly. "And during this so-called date you found yourself in the defendant's motel apartment?"

"Yes," she choked.

"Where he . . ." a pause for effect ". . . had sexual relations with you?"

Heath bolted to his feet. "That's none of your damn business, you filthy-minded bastard!" he cried, deeply wounded.

There were several moments of confusion as the judge banged his gavel. "You're out of order, Mr. Tanner." Heath's lawyer pulled him down and hovered over him placatingly while the jury cast him covert malevolent glances. The prosecutor's ploy had worked, and judging by his smug expression of satisfaction, he was aware of how well. The jury suspected Heath of being a seducer of innocent young girls and now knew beyond a doubt that he had a violent temper, as he had plainly demonstrated that fact before their very eyes.

Waxing magnanimous, the prosecutor offered, "I'll withdraw the question, Your Honor." He turned to Shelby again. "And when he was finished . . ."

"Your Honor, I object to this insinuation." This time it was Heath's attorney breaking in, using a mild, rational tone that was almost apologetic.

"I'll rephrase, Your Honor." He cleared his throat meaningfully. "And afterward Mr. Tanner returned you to the movie theater, where your sister subsequently picked you up?" he asked.

Shelby managed another broken "Yes." Her face sheened with tears, her innocent eyes beseeching, she turned to the jury silently, pleading wordlessly for Heath, not knowing that she was capturing their sympathy, pitting them even more firmly against him.

"The next time you saw the defendant was at the Driftwood Lounge, isn't that correct?"

Crying and nodding, she answered in the affirmative.

"And he bought you a drink."

She nodded again and her answer was a cracked sob.

"You saw Mr. Tanner have at least four drinks, didn't you?"

"Yes." She felt ill. Really ill. A dizzying nausea she fought to control.

"After which he tore into the victim in a savage rage? Merely because the poor unfortunate man showed you a little attention? The defendant became wildly angry, did he not? Assaulting Mr. Grossmann violently and beating him senseless. All because of his jealous lust for you! A mere seventeen-year-old girl!"

Pandemonium broke loose in the courtroom.

"Objection!" yelled the defense lawyer. "The witness can only answer one question at a time."

Shelby sobbed openly, making a beautiful picture of pitiful misery.

"Objection sustained," the judge ruled.

The prosecutor hitched his thumbs in the pockets of his vest. "Miss Constantine," he continued, his voice dripping with false sympathy, "did you witness the defendant's attack on Mr. Grossmann at the Driftwood Lounge?"

"Yes." Shelby managed this one syllable before completely breaking down and burying her face in her hands. The courtroom buzzed. The judge banged his gavel and asked if there would be cross-examination. Heath conferred quietly with his lawyer.

"We're waiting for the cross-examination," the judge pronounced irritably.

"I have no questions to ask of this witness," Heath's lawyer choked out reluctantly.

She had looked at Heath with naked love as she walked back to her seat. But a chiseled hatred had been his answering expression. He had spared her the humiliation of having the truth dragged out of her by forceful cross-examination. He had remained true to the very end, a protector, a gentleman rogue. She loved him with every pulsebeat of her young girl's heart. And what had she done for him? Nothing. She hadn't even tried to explain the truth.

When the jury came back with the verdict of guilty, she was stunned, grief-stricken. This wasn't the way her father had promised it would go. Heath was sentenced for aggravated assault.

As she drifted into an uneasy sleep, she saw his tall masculine form being led out of her life and taken to the place where she had sent him. She screamed and screamed until it seemed her head would burst from the intense pressure. And so her brief nightmare ended—with screams of anguish.

CHAPTER TWO

"Heath! Heath!" Desperate shrieks rose over the noise of the plane's engines.

"What's wrong with her?" Aaron looked back at their writhing cargo.

"She's having a nightmare," Joe Sam answered calmly.

"Did you hear who she called for?"

"Yes."

The two kidnappers looked at one another significantly.

"What do you make of it?" asked Aaron.

"I'm not sure."

"Heath!" Her scream pierced the air again.

"Go wake her up," Joe Sam ordered.

Aaron moved back into the passenger section and shook Shelby gently. Her eyes flew open in a wide uncomprehending stare. Cold sweat bathed her brow, and she was shaking uncontrollably.

"Wake up!" Aaron commanded. "You were dreaming."

She slumped against the back of the seat, exhausted. "Y-yes," she said shakily. "I know."

"Cigarette?" he offered.

"I don't smoke. But yes, I think I'll have one." She took the cigarette with trembling fingers and put it to her lips.

He lighted it, then got up to go back to his seat in the cockpit of the aircraft.

"Stay," she begged, blowing out a cloud of smoke. "I can't bear to be alone now."

He lounged back comfortably, giving her a curious look. "That must have been a terrible nightmare."

"Don't worry about it," she said caustically. "It happens all the time."

"Who is Heath?" he quizzed lowly, knowing that Joe Sam would not approve of this line of questioning.

"None of your business," she retorted, puffing on her cigarette nervously.

"He must have really been some guy to have made such a deep impression on you," Aaron went on, unable to resist fishing for information.

"He was. Let's drop it."

"Was?" Aaron raised his blond brows in a questioning manner.

"I haven't seen him in seven years."

"Yet you still dream about him? What is he? A long lost lover, or some kind of nemesis?"

"Both!" She stubbed out the cigarette viciously. "Who do you think you are anyway?" she asked angrily. "Perry Mason? You sound like a lawyer. I hate lawyers."

A flash of amusement crossed his face. "Sorry. I just wondered."

"Well, don't wonder about things that don't concern you. Oh, go back to your seat and leave me alone," she ordered crossly.

"Okay," he said agreeably. "I'm glad you're over your nightmare."

"I'm not over it. I'll never get over it," she said icily, then turned to look out the window.

He gave a brief, secretive smile and looked at the luminous numbers on his watch. "We'll be there in twenty minutes. We made good time. It only took eight hours."

"Where are we anyway?" she asked. "I can't see anything out there."

"Fifteen hundred miles from Florida—a long walk back."

"Very funny."

"You're an unusual woman," he remarked, appraising her keenly. "This kidnapping has frightened you, I know, but not nearly as much as that bad dream a few moments ago. How can you have such courage against us and shrivel up like a leaf in a bonfire over a dream of some man from your past?"

She gave him a wide honest stare and explained as if he were a simpleton, "Sometimes the tortures inside us are far more horrifying than those inflicted upon us by others."

His mouth dropped open in surprise and something akin to respect crept into his mild brown eyes. "Strange that you should say that. I know someone else in a similar predicament."

"Aaron," called Joe Sam, "we're coming in for a landing. Come here. It's tricky at night."

"Buckle your seat belt, Shelby," Aaron urged her kindly. And suddenly she knew with a comforting certainty that this blond young man with the gentle disposition had begun to like her.

Joe Sam piloted the plane to a neat stop on the short, dimly lit runway. They disembarked, and it seemed to Shelby that they had landed on a strip right in the middle of nowhere. The two men led her to a four-wheel-drive Scout. Joe Sam shoved it into low gear and took off over a bumpy, rutted terrain covered with tall grass. Shelby sat tensely, holding on to her seat as the jeep bounced through the black night toward a low dancing light in the distance.

The house in front of which they stopped was a well-proportioned two-story affair painted white. She couldn't see its details but had the distinct impression it had been recently built. They were obviously expected by someone, for the large white wooden front door was unlocked and a low light from a Tiffany lamp glowed in the front window.

Shelby sniffed new wood and fresh paint as she walked into a foyer tiled with rough uneven slabs of slate. Joe Sam led her into the spacious living room and motioned her to sit on a handsome leather couch.

"Mission accomplished," Aaron breathed in relief. "Will he want to see her this late? It's nearly three o'clock in the morning."

Joe Sam grunted. "I'll go check." He exited through a door leading to other parts of the house.

She looked down at herself and grimaced. In the soft light she could see that her stockings hung in threads, her arms were bruised and scratched, her skirt was a crumpled mess, and her blouse was beyond repair.

"A little worse for wear," Aaron agreed with her mute self-assessment, "but at least we got you here in one piece."

"No thanks to your Indian friend," Shelby retorted. "I thought for a while he was going to cut me up into a thousand tiny pieces."

Aaron laughed. "Joe Sam wouldn't have hurt you. He was bluffing and got away with it."

"I was sure murder was lurking behind that bronze mask he masquerades as a face."

28

Again Aaron laughed. "I assure you, Joe Sam is the kindest man alive. And one of the cleverest I've ever met. His poker face serves him well. Knowing you a little better now, I doubt if you would have come so peaceably with us if he hadn't put some fear into you."

"Aaron," she asked pleadingly, "what is this all about?"

He shook his head and refused to answer her.

Joe Sam walked noiselessly across the thick rust-colored carpet. "Take her to the red guest room. White Brave will see her in the morning." Turning to Shelby, he urged, "Sleep late, Summer Sky. No one will disturb you."

At that moment the weary, disheveled woman would have given a month's wages to know what thoughts and feelings were percolating behind Joe Sam's stoic Indian countenance.

Aaron led her up stairs that were padded with the same brownish-orange carpet, opened a dark walnut door that led off the hall, and flipped on a light. The scene was a gorgeously furnished room done in crimson, black, and white. Aaron placed her luggage on a low white dresser, gave her a friendly wave, exited, and turned the lock.

What luxury! She took off her battered pumps and wiggled her toes. Such red carpet treatment for a mere hostage! She looked around wonderingly. Having read accounts of kidnappers who shoved hostages into horrible closets and such, she felt extremely fortunate to have this opulence at her fingertips. This room was almost as large as the whole of her tiny apartment and much grander.

She slipped out of her skirt and blouse, pulled off the remains of her panty hose, and left the lot in a heap on the floor. Stumbling over to the king-size bed, she flung herself across its red satin spread, curled up into a defensive fetal

29

position, and forgot her plight long enough to fall into an exhausted, fretful sleep.

She awoke to soft sunlight filtering through sheer white draperies appliquéd with lace snowflakes. No sound from outside the room assaulted her ears. She lay motionless for a few moments, allowing her wide curious eyes to rove over the room at will, taking in the red wallpaper with its raised velvety fleur-de-lis, the many mirrored folding closet doors, the white, cool, shiny furniture, the two large windows with their diamond-shaped panes.

Was this lovely haven to be her cell for the length of her imprisonment? She moved off the bed, padded noiselessly to one of the windows, and pulled back the expensive fabric that curtained it. The beauty of a majestic mountain range greeted her gaze—white-capped peaks glistening in a clear turquoise sky, red and gray and ocher rocks jutting through the early snow, dark timberland winding in uncertain patterns, silver streams and rivulets threading here and there. A narrow golden grass field met the timberline and separated it from the orchard of fruit trees whose rows reached clear up to the back of the house.

These were not the familiar citrus trees she was so accustomed to. She could see glimpses of red showing through deep lush leaves flowing in the wind. Apples or pears, she suspected. She squinted at the mountains, realizing she had seen such grandeur only in pictures of the Rockies. And wasn't that where Aaron had told Mrs. Eversole they were taking her? How nice, she thought wryly. She had wanted to see them ever since Heath had told her that was where he was from.

Had he gone back to his home in Montana after being released from prison? She doubted it. He was a man with

30

the wanderlust. When she met him he had done construction work in nearly every part of the country.

His having a degree in political science had impressed her, but he had thought nothing of it. She wondered through the years just what he had wanted out of life. Getting a college education had apparently not satisfied him. He had wanted to see life, experience it, hence his carefree wanderings around the country. He had coveted his freedom, even gloried in it. She shook her head sadly. Well, she had taken care of all that. How could a man as independent as Heath have withstood being locked up?

His handsome image of brawny American independence was still imprinted indelibly in her mind. He had been a block layer. His huge biceps flexed easily as he had put one block upon another, troweling off excess mortar oozing from between. She had watched him in fascination, not caring that he hated her to hang around the construction site.

"You do very neat work."

"I try," he answered, grinning. His long, thick, almost black hair glinted cinnamon highlights as it curled wetly on a perspiring muscular neck. Her young heart had lurched crazily every time he favored her with one of his even, intensely white smiles. He was outstandingly good-looking and possessed all the easy grace that comes with knowing it.

He paused in his work, allowing his humorous black gaze to rake over her creamy shoulders and rest on the cleft between her breasts. "Run along, kid. You've got every man on the job gawking at you with his tongue hanging out."

"I'm not a kid. I'm twenty years old." This was a bald

lie, but she thrust out her ample bust as visible proof of her maturity.

He laughed. "Get lost. I don't care how old you are. Your coming around here every day is going to cost me my job. The boss doesn't like bystanders hanging around; they could get hurt." He reached for another block, moving comfortably and effortlessly within his bronzed shirtless skin.

"You have very wide shoulders," she said, mesmerized by his well-built body. "Did you get your muscles from lifting blocks?"

He shook his head. "I grew up on a ranch in Montana. During the summer we put up hay. Each bale weighed sixty-five pounds." He grabbed another block as if it were a Tinkertoy. "I used to throw two hundred bales a day."

Shelby silently calculated. "That's over six tons!"

"You must have made high grades in arithmetic." He chuckled. "Now go on before the boss comes back from his coffee break."

"I will on one condition."

"What?" He straightened, resting huge muddy hands on slim, faded jeans.

"That you ask me out." She wouldn't have believed herself capable of such raw aggressiveness, but once her desire was verbalized she refused to withdraw the suggestion or the boldness in her blue eyes.

"You're just begging for it, aren't you?" He laughed softly. He rested his weight on one foot in an arrogant pose. "If I take you out, will you promise never to come around here again?"

"Yes."

"You've got a deal. Where do you want to go?"

She gulped. He really meant it. She never dreamed he would really . . .

"How about a movie?" he suggested, cutting in on her confusing thoughts.

"Fine." She had at last found her voice.

"Where do you live?"

Now she *was* startled, and a little frightened. Her father would never condone her dating this mature and obviously very experienced man. "I'll meet you," she said quickly. "In front of the Plaza."

"Afraid your family won't approve of me?" he taunted.

"No. It's not that," she said, trying to sound casual. "It's just that my father won't be home tonight anyway, and . . . and I have a car of my own. So there's no need for you to make a trip to pick me up."

"Well, I do get off late on Fridays," he admitted. "Okay. Be at the movies tonight at seven."

She nodded and gave him an excited grin, suddenly feeling overwhelmed and a little shy.

"Go on now, and let me get back to work." He had spoken roughly, but a smile had caressed his coal-black eyes.

Shelby moved away from the window, allowing the soft white drapery to fall back into place. What a young stupid fool she had been seven years ago. What had driven her to tell such lies?

She jumped nervously at the knock at the door. "Just a minute," she called. Moving quickly to one of her suitcases, she unsnapped its clasps and opened it. She took a cotton shift from its jumbled contents and quickly put it on. "Come in."

A tall, slender young woman with long brown braids walked in carrying a breakfast tray. "You're to eat this," she muttered coldly, moving across the room on silent cat feet and setting the tray on the dresser. "White Brave expects you downstairs in an hour."

She was beautiful, with an olive-toned complexion and large, dark almond-shaped eyes which held a bottomless treasure of glittering hatred as they rested on Shelby's startled face.

"Thank you," Shelby responded, trying for a modicum of courtesy.

The young woman's lips curled. "So you are Shelby Constantine." She spat the name as if it tasted bitter in her mouth.

"So I am," Shelby answered, bristling defensively at her rudeness.

"Don't get smart with me," she menaced. "I would dearly love to kill you. I can't imagine why my grandfather didn't sink his knife into your overdeveloped bosom last night."

"So you're Joe Sam's granddaughter," Shelby surmised, turning sarcastic. "And you're in this little game too, along with the mastermind White Fang."

"Brave," the Indian woman corrected. "His name is White *Brave.*" Her voice was trembling with rage.

"Oh yes," Shelby minced caustically, "the indomitable phantom White Brave. Your husband, I presume? You probably make a lovely couple."

"He's my brother," she corrected through clenched teeth.

"Well isn't that nice," Shelby went on relentlessly. "A whole family of cutthroats. I'm sure you'll make a beautiful family portrait on the wanted posters."

At once the young woman sprang on Shelby like a sleek cat, hissing and spitting invective. Surprised, Shelby rolled under her attack, clawing back frantically in self-defense. The door burst open, and Joe Sam was pulling them apart and dragging them to their feet. The women were heaving and glaring hatefully at one another.

"Go downstairs, Dove," Joe Sam ordered.

The Indian woman left noiselessly. Shelby gingerly nursed a scratch on her arm. "Dove!" she burst out furiously. "What a laugh! That woman has the talons of a vulture and the teeth of a vampire."

Joe Sam looked at Shelby with her wild, blue-black hair, flushed cheeks set in creamy pallor, and bright sapphire eyes blazing blue fire.

"Pull yourself together and come on down. Don't cause any more trouble," he ordered through stiff, expressionless lips.

But Shelby was beside herself with rage and confusion. "Get out of my sight, you evil old man!" she screamed. "And the next time you sic that vicious little squaw on me, I'll claw her eyes out!"

Joe Sam merely stood before her like a wooden statue. Shelby turned away like a frenzied animal in a trap. "I'll fight you," she shrieked. "Don't expect me to submit meekly to this crazy kidnapping. I'll fight!"

"You won't fight anybody," a deep, resonant voice spoke from behind her. An unforgettable voice which shook her more than anything had thus far.

She stood rooted to the spot, staring unseeingly at the lacy snowflake curtains. It couldn't be. Heath couldn't be standing behind her now. She shook her head dumbly. He just couldn't be. She wouldn't turn around to see. How could she face this wonderful man of her dreams and nightmares?

"Get dressed," he ordered in tones edged with ice.

35

"Then eat your breakfast. I'll be waiting for you in my office." A brief silence. "And don't ever verbally or physically abuse one of my family again." His cruel inflection cut through her like a two-edged dagger.

The door slammed behind her and the lock clicked. It was only then that she allowed herself to move, and with the movement came a flood of weeping—an hysterical, silent waterfall which made her eyes sting and her throat constrict convulsively.

Stumbling to the adjoining bathroom, she twisted gold-plated knobs above an elegant oval tub and leaned over to support her body on weak arms. Stupid with shock, she watched the tub fill. Then she undressed mechanically and slid into its warm depths. What a pity she didn't have enough courage to go ahead and drown herself.

So it was Heath who was behind this hideous abduction. Just hearing the sound of his voice had brought powerful, poignant memories flooding back to torment her.

They had gone to the movies that night. He had teased her about choosing a Walt Disney production instead of something more adult. She had hardly touched her popcorn or barely seen the comical scenes enacted before her, she was so enchanted by his nearness. She stole covert glances at his dark profile and trembled with excitement and a strange desire she had never before known.

She had taken pains to look older that night, wearing white hugging slacks with a matching top that strained across her full bosom. The white of her suit and the creaminess of her skin contrasted nicely with her extravagant head of long velvet black hair. She had heard men like long hair. And she desperately wanted Heath to like her, to love her.

As the movie played across the screen in deep vibrant

multicolor, she indulged in romantic fantasies. Heath would fall in love with her. She would tell him she was only seventeen. He would wait for her to graduate from high school and they would get married. Or she would quit school and marry him. School, her father—nothing mattered except Heath, and being with him.

"Why are you so quiet?" he whispered in her ear. "Sorry, after all, that you came out with me?"

"No," she answered quickly. She turned to face him, her breath catching sweetly with his. "I-I've always wanted this . . . To be with you."

He slipped a large muscular arm around her flawless shoulders and moved closer. Their lips were nearly touching. "You're beautiful," he whispered. "You take my breath away."

Gazing into his soft black eyes, she saw something that made her feel helpless yet powerful.

"Enjoying the picture?" he asked, moving away.

"Yes . . . no . . . I mean I'm not really watching it."

"Neither am I. Would you like to go for a drive?"

That drive had led them to the motel where he rented a small efficiency apartment.

Shelby sobbed as she pulled herself out of the tub and stepped onto red carpeting, grabbing at the same time a plush white towel. Heath had been reluctant to take her there. She had suggested it, knowing that going to her house was out of the question yet not being willing to let the stolen evening with him end so soon.

She rubbed her body roughly with the towel as she shook her aching head. Looking back, she didn't think that either one of them had been aware of the magic drawing them together that night. Heath was a virile man, and as such, an opportunist, but she was firmly convinced

37

that he had not taken her to his room that night planning to seduce her. It was her own naïve forwardness that had fanned the spark between them into something towering and all consuming.

"Here it is," he had announced grandly as he flipped on the dim kitchenette light. "Humble, but home for the present."

"It's very nice," she commented, sinking onto his bed and scuffing off her sandals. One of her childish habits was to shed her shoes anywhere and everywhere, for in Florida barefoot was the only way to be. She crossed her legs under her and gave him a frank, open smile which must have seemed an obvious come-on.

"Are you sure you don't mind coming here?" he asked uncertainly. "After all, this is only our first date."

"Oh, I've seen motel rooms before." She shrugged nonchalantly, thinking of the vacations she had gone on with her parents before her mother had died. She shook her long hair down her back provocatively.

He turned, running his fingers through dark cinnamon-tinted hair. "This is going too fast even for me."

"Don't you want me here?" she asked in a small, hurt voice.

"Only if you're very, very sure," he answered in a deep voice that trembled slightly as he walked toward her.

"Oh I'm sure, Heath. I want to be with you more than anything in the world."

He sat on the bed regarding her incredulously. "Have you been in many motel rooms like this?"

"Oh sure. I've never been in one with a kitchen in it . . . but it must be a great luxury to be able to have coffee first thing in the morning."

He was startled. "You really have been around, haven't you?"

"Some." She smiled and her soft, luminous eyes melted over his features sensuously as she ached for something she had never known and couldn't define. "May I touch you?" she pleaded, reaching out shyly.

Thin tensile strands of desire whipped out to pull them together, binding them in a close, breathless kiss. Even now, looking back, she couldn't clearly remember how everything had happened from that moment on. Time had stood still—all conscious thought had fled. She had become a being of impulses and senses, experiencing for the first time a man's deep kisses, expert caresses. She was swept into a languorous ecstasy—a relentless tide that shattered the breath and set the body adrift on a sea of pure sensation. Perhaps if he had been rougher or had rushed her she would have become frightened and pulled away.

But he had been slow, tender, deliberate. He had savored every taste, every exploring, all-consuming kiss. Every caress had been a study in motion and tactile fascination; each soft murmur against her skin a drugging, soothing symphony. He smelled of earth and rain-washed sunshine and evening grass freshly mowed.

She had responded under his lovemaking as a woman of experience, giving, moving to meet every touch, her love kindling and instinctively knowing the way.

A certain visual remembrance of that night later haunted dreams that were not nightmares. She was looking down through a warm hazy glow, watching him as he slowly and with sweet precision lifted her breast and drew its tender, rose-pleated nipple into his mouth—a masculine mouth that moved languidly to pull and suckle.

39

Then he had overspread her like a loving angel and she had sprawled instinctively to receive him, crying out, but not stiffening or trying to retreat.

"My God, you're a virgin." All movement stopped and he buried his face in her neck, his body quivering as a dam on the verge of bursting.

"Don't leave me," she begged, fearing his abandonment as the ultimate pain. She pressed her palms in the dents of his hips and moved against him.

"Stop." His breath caught and his heart thundered against her breasts. "This is all wrong."

"Please," she whispered. "Please."

He prayed inaudibly, but even while doing so he was already surrendering, thrusting himself forward, taking them both to the highest reaches of ecstasy, and to an unforgettable and matchless fulfillment.

Afterward she lay quietly and watched his expression turn from peace to self-disgust. He rolled to the edge of the bed, then rose to dress. He brought a warm washcloth and swabbed her tenderly, helping her, with gentle hands, get back into the white pantsuit.

That done, he moved to the far reaches of the room and prowled restlessly, his gentleness turning to confusion and anger.

"Explain!" he finally exploded.

"I-I don't know what you mean." Her face slowly crumpled.

"Don't cry," he ordered sternly. "I couldn't stand it."

Bravely, she pulled herself together, her eyes shimmering with unshed tears. He was struck forcibly by her childish innocence. He turned away and raked his fingers through his hair in extreme agitation.

"How old are you, Shelby?" he asked fearfully. "Really."

"Seventeen," was her squeaky answer.

Cursing bitterly, he slammed his fist against the wall. "Seventeen! I have a kid sister your age. Not even out of high school. I'll burn in hell for this!"

"I'm very mature for my age."

"You sure as hell are. You're also a very good liar!" The force of what he had done hit him squarely between the eyes. He staggered to the foot of the bed like a felled animal and slumped down weakly.

"I . . . I'm sorry. Don't be mad." She crawled over and touched his shoulder.

"Get away from me!"

She drew back, deeply hurt, her eyes spilling over. He jerked her from the bed and shoved her purse into her midriff.

"You're going home, pronto!"

"I-I lied about having a car," she snuffled.

"That doesn't surprise me in the least. God, I've been dumb. How were you planning to get home?" He steered her out the door and into the glare of a brightly blinking neon sign.

"My sister is supposed to pick me up at eleven o'clock in front of the picture show."

He glanced at his watch. "Fifteen minutes." He tossed her in the car and slammed the door in her face. Revving up quickly, he screeched off toward the Plaza. He couldn't get rid of her soon enough.

Shelby's tempered flared. She was a stubborn girl, with a lot of pride. "You're acting like a maniac."

"Shut up. Don't you have any idea of what just happened?"

"I'm glad it did," she said defiantly.

"You little idiot! Go find a pimply-faced high school kid to have an affair with. This sort of thing isn't my style." He brought the car to a lurching stop in front of the Plaza, leaned across her, and opened the door. "Get out! And stay away from me. You're dynamite."

She got out mechanically and his car sped off with a muffled roar. He must have driven around the block, for a moment later he pulled up about half a block away and waited until her sister picked her up. He had apparently been worried about her being alone on a dark street so late at night.

Shelby forced her mind back to the present. She crossed the red carpet to her luggage and pawed around in search of something to wear. She found a sapphire blue pantsuit of soft jersey knit that wasn't too crushed. Aaron and Joe Sam had done a poor job of packing. She noticed hordes of pants and tops but no underthings.

She dressed with the jerky movements of a robot, then sat before the mirror wondering if anything could be done about her tear-ravaged face. A cold washcloth might take down some of the swelling in her puffy eyelids.

What would Luann say if she knew Heath had swept her forcibly back into his life? Shelby placed the cold cloth against her flushed face. Luann had always wanted her and Heath to meet again. She had some notion that Shelby's encountering him again face to face would somehow heal old wounds of guilt and hate. Shelby couldn't see how this could be possible. Her sister was a romantic, having experienced only smooth sailing with her husband, Woody. Nothing could come of this present situation with Heath but more heartbreak and pain. He hated her unreservedly. She had felt the searing hatred in his voice. Hatred she deserved.

Dry-eyed and finally in control, the stunned woman took her makeup bag from her purse and began the ritual of fixing her face, a young delicate face of fine bones and pure eggshell skin, tinted only faintly with the peach of a lingering Florida tan.

If only she had left Heath alone after that night. But she had been determined to see him again, to convince him that she really loved him as a woman and not just as a mixed-up, infatuated child.

She had stayed away a week, until her need drove her to the construction site. She had remained hidden until he got off work. She knew better than to follow him into that bar, but she was compelled.

Hips swaying seductively, slender straight back held proudly, and bust lifted to a prominent angle, she went through the smoke-filled room to where he was sitting on a stool, his wide-wedged back hunched comfortably over a mug of beer.

"Hi," she said cheerily, hopping on to the stool beside him.

"Are you nuts?" he asked in a stiff, shocked voice.

A squat, perspiring bartender in a white apron rolled up to ask her pleasure.

"A margarita, please," she ordered easily. "On the rocks."

The fat man didn't bat an eye as he waddled away then came back in a moment with her drink. She gave Heath a triumphant look. He downed his beer and ordered another while throwing the money for her drink on the counter.

"So what have you proved?" he challenged, pulling the foam moustache from his upper lip.

"Only that I can order a drink without being asked for an ID."

The bartender slid a beer down the counter to Heath. He caught it and took a long swig. "Big deal. Now run along home and tuck yourself in with your teddy bear."

"No." She lifted her drink to take a sip.

"You're not going to drink that!" he snapped, grabbed it from her hand, and polished it off in three gulps. Then he shuddered and chased it with the rest of his beer. "Another," he called to the bartender.

"Tequilla mixed with beer is a potent combination," she said wisely.

"How do you know so damn much about booze?" he slurred.

"My father is retired military—a veteran drinker."

He sipped on his fresh mug. "Go away, Shelby. You don't impress me with this grown-up act."

"Would it impress you if I told you I love you?" she asked almost inaudibly. She reached out to run her fingers lightly through the dark hairs across the back of his hand. "I really do. I love you, Heath."

His gaze penetrated the depths of her bright blue eyes. He shook his head slowly as if in a trance. "Are you crazy? Or am I? I can't tell." Then: "I'm drinking too much . . . too fast." He gulped down the foamy liquid that had almost a greenish cast in the strange, dim light. Then he set the empty mug back on the counter with a thud. "I'm leaving tomorrow. I've quit my job."

"No!" she cried.

"Yes."

"Because of me?"

He examined the bottom of his empty glass. "Every time I think of you I'm ashamed of what I am thinking. You're trouble, Shelby. Big trouble."

She was raw and bruised. He didn't want her; he was going away. She was uncannily mature enough to have a woman's pride, and that pride was now in the dust.

"Hi, Heath old buddy." A red-haired, uncouth-looking man slapped him on the back.

"Hi, Ralph," he responded tonelessly.

"Who's your girlfriend?" He turned his flushed, mottled face and beery breath on Shelby. "What's your name, sweetie?"

"Leave her alone, Ralph," Heath menaced, clenching his fists.

"Oh come on, pal. You can't have her all to yourself."

"Leave her be. She's just a baby."

"A very pretty baby," he complimented obscenely. "How about letting Ralph buy you a little ole drink over there at that nice quiet table?" he urged Shelby persuasively.

It was then that she made a horrible error in judgment. She was just too inexperienced to realize that Heath was so tense, so near the breaking point. She had wanted to make him a little jealous, that's all, not goad him into a wild protective rage.

"I think I'll accept your offer, Ralph." She smiled and slid to her feet, revealing the inside of one shapely thigh. "Heath doesn't care for my company."

Heath unfolded himself off his stool like a tightly wound coil ready to spring. "If you lay a hand on her," he warned Ralph, "I'll bust your head wide open."

People had begun to gather around. Shelby became frightened. Ralph merely laughed and pulled her by the arm. Heath sprang with lightning swiftness, smashing his huge bear paw fist into Ralph's unsuspecting face. Shelby screamed as Ralph spun around crazily like a child's top and crashed his temple into the corner of a table before hitting the floor.

The rest was a nightmare of flashing lights and uniformed police officers. Her father told her the next day that Ralph was in the hospital with a severe concussion. Heath was in the county jail.

It was all so tragic. Heath would blame himself, but she knew the whole horrible catastrophe had been her fault.

Coming back to the present, she suddenly realized that she must have been holding her lipstick wand in suspended animation for some time. Quickly smearing on the coral color, she surveyed the results of her efforts. Terrible. Face too pale, eyes too wide, mouth too startlingly bright.

She moved over to the tray of food Heath's sister had brought and turned sick at the sight of cold scrambled eggs and dry, shriveled toast. But the coffee in the thermal carafe was still warm. She poured a cup and gulped it greedily, hoping in vain for a miracle revival.

There was a knock at the door. It was Aaron. "May I come in?"

"Certainly."

"Are you ready?"

"No."

"Come along, Shelby. He's waited a long time."

She thrust out her chin bravely and followed Aaron, her legs feeling like putty.

46

CHAPTER THREE

Aaron stood behind her in front of the huge oak door that led to Heath's office. She paused and cast him a frantic searching look over her shoulder. "Will you come with me?"

"No."

"Throwing me into the lion's den?" she asked with a wry twist of her mouth.

"I . . . I'm sorry."

"So am I. Dreadfully, dreadfully sorry. Do you hate me as much as the rest of them do?"

"No."

"Thank you." She twisted the doorknob and walked into the room—a proud, beautiful woman emanating dignity and a fighting spirit.

He stood in jeans and a western shirt, making a huge hulking silhouette against a bright sunlit bay window. He still had the same wide back, tapering into a muscular waist and hard, powerful hips.

When she closed the door firmly behind her, he didn't turn from the window. Did he dread this confrontation as much as she did? Impossible.

"Have a seat, Shelby," he offered in a polite, well-modulated voice.

"Thank you." She arranged herself tautly in a stiff brown leather chair.

A shaft of sunlight fell across her face, showing flawless pearlescent complexion. She was pale but composed. The mad gush of tears beforehand had been a private affair. No need for hysterics here in front of Heath. He would come around to making his point soon enough.

He turned around and prowled over to his desk, shuffling and rearranging papers. His large capable hands caught her attention—strong, thick, clean—hands that had gently caressed her so long ago.

She let out a ragged breath and focused on his face. Cold, glittering eyes regarded her steadily. His straight hair, worn shorter now, was still very dark with subtle shades of auburn, framing a face partially covered with a well-shaped beard and moustache the startling color of cinnamon—a fiery contrast to his thick, dark hair.

"You haven't changed much," he began cuttingly. "But then you were a full-grown woman in many ways seven years ago."

"Why have you brought me here?" she challenged softly, flinching at the cold hatred in his black eyes. "Revenge?"

"What makes you call it revenge?"

"What else?"

"Justice, perhaps. I'm a man of law now. I studied law in prison and obtained my degree just after being released." He moved restlessly from behind his desk to a wall lined with shelves upon which sat volumes of large ponderous leatherbound books. "You are guilty of a heinous crime—that of murdering a man's freedom. I hate to see such a crime go unpunished."

"I can see that you hate," she said, clutching her hands

in front of her. "It oozes out of your pores like venom and nearly paralyzes me."

"Do you deny that you deserve it?" he asked harshly. "Surely you don't mean to put in a plea of innocence."

"Of course I'm guilty," she agreed tremulously.

"As guilty as Delilah." He shot her a tense, black look and she nearly broke into a million pieces. "You lured me on, wouldn't leave me alone, drove me to violence, then allowed a slick attorney to railroad me with lies and innuendos without even trying to explain the truth."

"I'm sorry."

"That's not enough. You must pay."

"Don't you even want to hear my side? I suffered too."

He gave a low, mirthless laugh, "You suffered! What kind of line are you trying to feed me? You went on merrily to become a ravishing party girl. You suffered! What a laugh! You had a high time while I rotted inside a locked cell!"

"Please listen to me, Heath. Even the worst criminal is given the chance to offer a defense."

"You have no defense. The facts condemn you," he broke in vindictively. "You're a cheat and a liar and you have the morals of an alley cat."

She knew then that trying to explain her young foolish love for him would be futile. He didn't want to listen to reason. He didn't want to hear about the trouble she had gone through with her father or the hideous guilt that had haunted every day and night of her life since the trial.

"I can see that you are judge and jury all rolled into one. At last I am your prisoner, but I'm sure there is not a shred of mercy within you, so I won't try to plead my case. God only knows what I've gone through—and perhaps my sister."

"Don't snivel," he ordered caustically. "It doesn't become you."

She raised her chin defiantly and asked, "What are you going to do with me, Heath? Browbeat me? Or just beat me?" A tinge of sarcasm edged into her voice. "How about fifty lashes? But that's not enough, is it? What about tying me to a stake and . . ."

"Shut up," he commanded harshly. "I'm sentencing you to a year in prison."

"You're serious, aren't you?" She gave him a wide, startled stare, her eyes blue splashes in a stark matte-white face. "Don't be absurd!"

"A little unusual, but ingenious, don't you think?" Even teeth flashed whitely through his beard. "It was my grandfather's idea. You are to spend a year in isolation, far from the excitement of your wild parties and amorous boyfriends."

"You won't get away with it! My boss will report my disappearance to the police; my sister will not rest until I am found. Oh, Heath!" she wailed. "I couldn't bear to see you go to prison again—for this!"

"My clever grandfather counted on that," he said as he took his seat behind the huge oak desk. Lancing his fiery beard into steepled fingers, he chuckled mirthlessly.

Suddenly Shelby realized the strength of the iron cage he had dropped around her; her breath seemed to leave her body. He knew she would never incriminate him for this. Going through another trial and watching him being sent off to prison again was unthinkable. Any fate would be preferable to that. No, Heath was safe in this outlandish plot for revenge, for revenge it was no matter what else he had called it. The plan was diabolically clever, for she would never report him for kidnapping.

"You will call your sister and tell her that you have met up with me again and that I have offered you a fantastic job. Lead her to believe that a flame of romance has been rekindled between us, if you think she'll believe it . . ."

"Oh, she'll believe it," Shelby cut in. "Your wicked grandfather is very sly, and you seem to take after him admirably."

He rose to a threatening height. "Watch out, Shelby. I don't intend to harm you, but just watch your mouth."

She retreated in the large leather chair in fascination. He had become a man of frightening dimensions, different from the cocky, self-assured block layer she had fallen in love with so long ago. "My job," she said weakly. "Mr. Tate will not understand. He thinks a great deal of me."

Heath waved a hand at this small detail. "Aaron Tate has taken care of that."

"Aaron who?" she asked dumbly.

"Aaron Tate, my law partner and friend." Heath laughed, savoring her helpless confusion. "Your boss is his father."

"Mr. Tate is Aaron's father? This is unbelievable."

"How do you think I knew where to find you? It was Aaron who told me about you after a recent trip home to visit his father, who couldn't stop praising his new private secretary named Shelby Constantine. Aaron recognized your name immediately and seemed fascinated that you were the same woman whose damaging testimony helped send me to prison."

"So Aaron helped you and Joe Sam cook up this neat little scheme to abduct me?" Shelby asked. "Does Mr. Tate know I'm here?" she asked.

"He thinks you'll be working for us in our law practice in Butte."

"Mr. Tate wouldn't give me up just like that. He likes my work."

"And that's not all," Heath remarked roughly as he sat down on the edge of his desk with easy grace.

"What filthy thing are you implying?" she shot back. "There's nothing between Mr. Tate and me."

He gave her a withering look of disbelief. "Aaron's mother is deathly afraid of you. She wants her niece to have your job. A niece—so much safer than the office bombshell, the beautiful, wild party girl who has every man in the firm turning flips to go out with her."

Shelby's hands, slippery from perspiration, squeezed the leather-padded arms of the chair.

"Dexter Tate," Heath went on, "seemed quite relieved when Aaron suggested that you come out here to work for us. It was a good solution to his dilemma. I'm sure it got his wife off his back immediately. Aaron told him that he had spoken to you at length and that you were looking forward to coming out west."

"Mr. Tate would have asked me himself. He wouldn't have just transferred me without talking it out first."

"He was supposed to talk to you next week, but we couldn't allow that, could we?" Heath asked easily. "Aaron will call him today and give him some story about how we needed you out here immediately."

"This is insane. I feel so helpless . . . so trapped!"

"Exactly," he responded with satisfaction as he took a cigarette out of a gold embossed case on his desk. He lighted it, inhaled deeply, and calmly blew smoke toward the ceiling.

"You've changed," she accused.

"Of course." He examined the tip of his cigarette dispassionately. "Prison has a way of doing that to a man. Go to your room. Lunch will be brought to you at twelve thirty."

"You can't really mean to keep me locked upstairs in that room for a whole year!" she cried.

"No," he answered. "I wouldn't have you living in the same house with me. After lunch I'll take you to your . . ." he hesitated ". . . cell. Now get out of here. I've seen enough of you for the moment." His hand trembled imperceptibly as he again lifted the cigarette to his mouth.

Dazed, she hurried up the stairs to her room. Flinging the door open, she ran to the window, unlocked it, and threw up the sash in a frenzy for oxygen, for she felt as if she were suffocating. The air wafting down from the high mountains in the distance was rare and cool. She breathed it deeply in great gulps.

"Don't jump," came a wry, toneless voice from behind.

She turned to face the cold, frozen form of Joe Sam. "I wouldn't give Heath that satisfaction!" she exclaimed hotly. "How long have you been standing there, you old sneak?" She whispered this, knowing that if Heath heard her railing his grandfather again he would very likely toss her out the window, making a quick and final end to her.

"Long enough to see that your first meeting with my grandson after so many years has left you very breathless and shaken," Joe Sam replied coolly.

"I suppose that gives you a great deal of satisfaction," she said, striding from the window to the dressing table, where she grabbed her brush and began attacking her long hair with swift vicious strokes.

"Yes, I'm glad to see that you are a woman of some feeling after all," he grunted.

"I understand you masterminded this sick scheme," she offered in mock congratulations. "How you and Heath will enjoy watching me squirm! But I assure you, I will not break down into piteous hysterical pleading," she announced, on the verge of doing just that. "Sorry to disappoint you. I know that would please you immensely."

"What pleases me is not important," he grunted. "I care only for my grandson."

"He's a monster!"

"He is a man torn by deep emotions. The memory of you has ravaged his mind for years like a great clawing animal, leaving pits of darkness within his soul."

"He hates me with a terrible vengeance!" she exclaimed, slamming the brush on the dresser in frustrated despair.

Joe Sam's eyes were hooded. "What he feels for you is strong," he agreed. "Strong enough to change him into something I don't want him to be. It has been painful to watch the transformation."

"His feelings about the past have been no less debilitating than my own." She gave the weatherbeaten Indian a wide, honest look in the mirror. "But you wouldn't have considered that aspect of it, would you? You don't care what all this might do to me."

"That's true." He held her stare. "I was thinking only of White Brave when I suggested this plan. However, now I see even better what a good plan it is, for you have your own hounds of hell chasing you. Isn't that right?"

"Yes, I have, but the fact remains that you brought me here to feed his hate." Slowly she walked toward the ancient Indian, then stopped to face him squarely. "I am guilty," she said quietly. "There are things you don't know about what happened seven years ago, and I'm sure you wouldn't be interested in hearing them. Heath wasn't. But

no extenuating circumstances can erase the guilt I feel about what I did. In a sense I deserve this ridiculous, diabolical arrangement. But don't," she flashed, "just don't expect me to offer myself up on a silver platter to be devoured by your grandson's hatred. He will not destroy me. I promise you that!"

"You are a very brave squaw. This is all so much more interesting than I ever dreamed it would be." He turned and walked to the door.

"You sadist!" she accused.

"Which reminds me," he added, turning slightly before leaving. "I've spoken to Dove. She will not molest you again."

"Well, isn't that just keen," Shelby sneered.

Within moments a tray of soup and sandwiches and a tall thermos of iced tea was brought to her by Dove, who walked in and out of the crimson room silently, only a snarling upper lip betraying her sentiments. As the terribly alone woman sat down to the tray, she hoped fervently that she would never encounter the vicious Dove alone on a dark night.

Shelby took two bites of a sandwich, and although the creamy chicken salad would have undoubtedly been delicious in other circumstances, she couldn't eat; every morsel stuck in her throat like a huge wad of sawdust. But the tea was good, sweet and lemony.

There was a knock at the door. Aaron's voice came through. "Change into a pair of jeans, Shelby. Then come on down again. You'll be leaving in about twenty minutes."

Fifteen minutes later she was walking through the wide deep living room toward Heath's office door, dressed in a faded pair of jeans she usually wore while cleaning her apartment. Aaron and Joe Sam had made such a mess of packing her clothes that all of her blouses were wrinkled accordian-style. She had chosen to put on a bright red T-shirt top, her shapely figure pressing out the few creases in it.

"Come in," Heath invited curtly at her knock. "Time to call your sister. Are you up to it?"

"Of course." Shelby crossed the room, reaching for the telephone. His fingers, strangely warm, closed around her hand like an iron vise.

"Don't make any mistakes, or you'll be mysteriously disconnected."

"I wouldn't dream of it," she replied coolly.

He released her, but the heat of his touch lingered, causing her to tremble secretly. The operator made the necessary connections over the miles of cable, and her sister's familiar voice came through clearly but distantly, as if she were speaking through a long tunnel.

"Luann?" Shelby said brightly, blinking back her tears. Here was the voice of one, perhaps the only one in the world, who truly loved her. She had written off her father a long time ago.

"Shelby, is that you? You sound so far away."

"I am, as a matter of fact." Shelby laughed as she looked up at the ceiling, biting her trembling lips. "I'm in Montana."

"Montana! My God! What are you doing there?"

"You won't believe my . . ." she swallowed thickly, " . . . good fortune. I've been offered the most fantastic job."

"You're going to work in Montana?" Luann asked incredulously.

"Yes, I flew out yesterday. By the way, will you go by my apartment and clean out my dishes and things? And

56

tell Mrs. Eversole to go ahead and rent my apartment to someone else. I think she's rather confused about the whole thing."

"But this is so sudden," Luann said doubtfully. "I don't like your being so far away."

"Oh, but it was an offer I couldn't refuse," she choked. "I'm private secretary for Heath Tanner. He is a lawyer now. His partner is Mr. Tate's son. They just had to have me out here," she rushed on.

Heath gave her a wry, mirthless smile.

"Shelby!" Luann exclaimed. "You're going too fast. Who did you say you are working for?"

"Heath Tanner."

There was dead silence over the line. Finally Luann breathed, "Heath Tanner! That must explain your strange tone of voice. I always told you he would bear you no grudges once you explained the whole story. Oh, Shelby, just think, you and Heath together again!"

"Yes," she replied, "just think." Heath made an impatient gesture with his hand. "I must go, Lu. This call is costing Heath a fortune. I'll write and explain it all."

"Heath Tanner," Luann said again as if her mind were stuck on his name. "Please write and tell me all about it. I want to know everything."

Sensing that the conversation must soon terminate and not wanting it to, Shelby hung on to the receiver fiercely, as it was the only contact she had with love. "How are Woody and the kids?"

"Woody is busy disking the grove, and there's layers of dust in the house. Joanie got a big wad of bubble gum stuck in her hair, and I had to cut it out, which left an awfully funny-looking gap. Jeffie is giving his first grade teachers a run for their money. When I ask them how he is doing, they just raise their eyes to heaven and comment tactfully that he is a very active child. So everything is fine here." She laughed. "The usual normal insanity."

"Oh yes." Shelby laughed shakily. "I'll miss that on Sundays." She clenched her teeth against an upsurging sob.

Heath made a karate chop with his hand, which she couldn't fail to catch the meaning of. "I have to go now." She leaned over the phone, still clutching the receiver as if it were a lifeline. "How is the weather there?" Heath snorted audibly.

"Hot! Unbearably hot. You sound funny. Are you sure you're okay?"

"Fine. Great. It's cool here. Super cool. Cold, in fact." Her face was inches from the phone now, and the receiver seemed glued to her ear. Heath's hand came into her line of vision and moved to push down the button which would cut them off. "'Bye, sis. I love you."

"Oh, Shell, me too."

"'Bye, sis."

The line went dead. Heath took the receiver and cradled it. Shelby turned and walked stiffly to the other side of the room, feeling as if she had just swallowed barbed wire. She would not break down; she simply would not give him the pleasure of seeing it.

"Remarkable," he said sardonically. "You are still one helluva liar. A brilliant performance." His deep voice was derisive. "If I had an Academy Award handy, I would present it to you immediately."

"Go ahead and torture me, Heath." She focused on him moist blue eyes which would have melted any other man into a pool of pity. "You're like a little boy with a fly in a jar."

"Butterfly," he corrected. "You're an exotic rare butterfly—cream and black and turquoise blue." He reached out and grabbed a handful of curving velvet black hair, pulling it so that her head was forced back. "So beautiful. And you speak so glibly of torture. I torture you? What a laugh!" His eyes were narrow black slits as they raked insultingly over her body.

"Let me go," she menaced through clenched teeth. "You've no right to touch me."

Grinding his teeth, he released her swiftly and led her out of the house to a high-roofed red barn a little distance away, where he busied himself saddling two horses. "We can't go in the jeep. Grandfather has taken it to Choteau for supplies, so I'll have to bring you your luggage later. Can you ride?"

"Yes. My brother-in-law bought horses for us when I lived with my sister. I like to ride."

"Us?" he questioned, raising heavy, formidable brows.

"My sister and I," she explained, "and her two children, although they were only big enough to have small ponies at the time."

"Your brother-in-law sounds like a generous man," he remarked, cinching his black stallion securely.

"Woody is a wonderful man. My sister's home is the only real home I've ever known."

"You don't get along well with State Representative Constantine, I take it," he said shortly.

"I haven't lived with Father for years. He never showed a great deal of affection toward either Luann or me. He loved his career—first military, then political."

"And your mother?"

"I don't remember her very well. She was a frightened, mouselike creature always scurrying to do Father's bid-

59

ding. She died while we were stationed in Spain. I think Luann was the only one who really grieved for her. I was too young, and Father . . . well, Father was Father—a hard, unyielding man." She shivered and hugged her soft suede jacket. "It's cold."

"It's not the least bit cold," he contradicted. "This is balmy compared to what it will be when winter sets in. Sometimes the snow drifts higher than a man's head."

"I've never seen snow—real snow," Shelby confessed.

"You'll get your fill of it in Montana." He patted the shiny flank of a chestnut mare and motioned her up with a wave of his hand. "Ready?"

She mounted agilely. "Where are we going?"

He nodded toward a shimmering magenta and white range in the distance before mounting his stallion with the grace of an accomplished horseman. "This way," he directed. "That yellow patch of tamarack at the foot of the mountain is our destination. You can barely see it from here."

She followed in silence, waiting, alert to his every movement. When would he turn his horse around and call this whole thing off? When would he admit it was all a fantastic practical joke and make arrangements for Joe Sam to take her back home?

The prairie rolled before them in a wide, undulating sea of buffalo grass. She saw a herd of cattle grazing off to one side. "What breed to you raise here?" she asked in an effort to dispel the unfriendly silence between them.

"Hereford. Whitefaces, we call them."

A cool wind played in her long, flowing curtain of blue-black hair. "Ranching must be very profitable, or did you build your beautiful house with money you made practicing law?"

"Nosy, aren't you?"

"Just curious. Of course it's none of my business," she conceded defensively.

"I do well with the cattle business, and we raise grain too. I've won myself a reputation as a good defense lawyer, but in the past year Aaron has taken over most of my practice. I still advise him on difficult questions, and he keeps me informed on the status of our current cases. Occasionally I help him in court, but not often. I much prefer being here on the ranch, especially during spring and fall, our busiest times in handling the cattle. But it was Grandfather who made our wealth; he is largely responsible for the fortune it took to build the house."

"Joe Sam!" she exclaimed.

"Yes. He has always been convinced that a section of our land about thirty miles from here covered deep reservoirs of petroleum. Standard Oil sent a man out to investigate a few years ago, when the fuel shortage scare started. To put it bluntly, we struck it rich."

Shelby was speechless. Heath was a man who had everything: success, material wealth, vast lands. He had come a long way from the cocky construction worker she had fallen in love with.

"Of course, it's nowhere near as large as the fields in Texas, but it's impressive."

Some of his antagonism toward her seemed to be evaporating in the brisk Montana wind, and although he wasn't friendly by any means, at least he wasn't hostile.

She pressed her advantage. "Tell me about your grandfather. He's the most unusual man I've ever met."

"Grandfather is a legend in these parts."

"How did he acquire all this land?"

"A man named Blocker used to own this ranch. He

hired Grandfather as his foreman. In those days, they ran over two thousand head here. He had an only child, a red-haired, fiery-tempered daughter who fell madly in love with Grandfather. You can guess the rest."

"They got married, inherited the ranch, and lived happily ever after," Shelby provided.

"That's close." Heath's open expression changed to a look of indifference. "They did get married, and they did inherit the ranch. But in those days people were terribly prejudiced toward Indians. An Indian was considered a crazy savage who would knife a man for a pint of whiskey. And the Blackfeet, my grandfather's tribe, were considered among the worst of the red men. My grandfather and grandmother had it plenty tough. They had more than the land and the elements to fight—they had to struggle against bigotry too. But they were strong. They survived."

"Her red hair certainly has." Shelby couldn't help getting in a dig.

He scratched his beard thoughtfully. "You don't like it? Dove says it doesn't match my hair."

She wasn't about to admit how handsome she thought he was. "It looks fine—even if it doesn't quite match."

He urged his horse to gallop, and Shelby followed close behind. They didn't speak again until they reached the thick timberland. Heath dismounted, and Shelby slid off her horse onto a carpet of yellow and ocher pine needles.

"You'll be staying in my grandparents' old place here among this stand of tamarack." He moved toward a small square log house that looked far from being habitable. "There used to be a bunkhouse just out on the prairie where fifteen or twenty cowboys lived, a corral over there," he indicated with a sweep of his hand to the right, "and hen houses and a barn just outside the timberline."

"Where do your ranch hands live now?" she asked, avoiding the old cabin like the plague.

"My foreman lives a few miles from here, in the frame house where I grew up. My hands are housed close to him." He strode toward the cabin. "Come on in and see your prison."

"Oh, Heath, you can't possibly be serious about this!"

"Of course I'm serious. Did you think that engaging me in a bit of idle chatter would change my mind?"

"You're despicable!" she burst out.

The cabin was dirty and drab inside. But its two rooms were large, and Shelby imagined that under the feminine ministrations of Heath's determined, red-haired grandmother the place might have once blossomed with hominess. But now—ugh! She wondered how many spiders lurked in the cobwebbed corners.

"How long has it been since anybody lived here?" she asked fearfully.

"About twenty-five years. My grandparents moved into the frame house to take care of Dove and me after our parents died," he explained.

"I see."

"But it's sturdy." He pounded a solid log in the wall with his fist. "It won't cave in under a snowdrift."

"How comforting." She said acidly. In her despair she had resorted again to sarcasm.

"And you have running water," he said, moving over to a small enamel sink, over which stood a large cast-iron pump of indeterminate age. The ancient handle squeaked alarmingly when he pushed it up and down. "Of course, you'll have to prime it to get it going. The well is out on the back porch."

"What luxury!"

63

He looked at her askance, and she could see by the malicious gleam in his deep black eyes that he was enjoying himself.

"Sorry there's no electricity," he apologized. She waved her hand at this triviality. "But there are lanterns and coal oil." He blew the dust off the glass chimney of a lantern, and Shelby held her nose to keep from sneezing. "And here's a wood stove for cooking and heating. That fireplace over against the wall," he commented, pointing to a vast brick cavern blackened with soot, "will also warm you nicely." He waved expansively. "Well, what do you think?"

She wanted to jump on him and claw his cruel black eyes out. She wanted to rant and rave and beat his chest hysterically. She could not live in this hole—no television, no radio, no people, no comforts. She nearly broke apart.

"Well?" he queried.

She gave him a sickly smile and used her only weapon—sarcasm. "It's lovely. The Waldorf-Astoria, no less."

He made one menacing step toward her, then turned on his heels and stalked out angrily, nearly tearing the slab door off its leather hinges. She ran to the window and saw him gallop by, a black flash of fury; and she felt the keenest sense of abandonment, for he was leading her chestnut mare behind.

She turned and surveyed her dismal surroundings and, to keep from sinking into total misery, went on a poking exploration. The room she was in contained, besides the large square black stove, a crude trestle table banked with split-log benches and a wide-backed rocker shoved into a corner beside an old dusty butter churn. That was all.

She thudded to the center of the desolate room on the

strong plank boards that made up the floor. No comfortable sofa, no deep easy chair. Perhaps the room had once contained these things, but not now. There was a door beside the stove that led into a small pantry, which contained a large stock of canned foods—meats, powdered milk, vegetables, fruits—and various packages of cereals and rice. There was a sparce supply of detergents and toiletries here too, set incongruously on a shelf above a tub of dirty potatoes.

After shutting this door, she opened the one that led to the other room of the cabin. It contained a wide bed and a fairly new looking chest of drawers. She walked over and pushed the mattress with splayed fingers to test its springiness, finding it firm. She lifted the attractive quilt coverlet and saw clean white sheets underneath. The bed was apparently new and the sheets freshly laundered. At least she would sleep comfortably, and she wouldn't starve to death.

A quilt in the corner covered a Singer sewing machine of ancient vintage—the pedal kind that operated on leg muscle power instead of electricity. She unfolded its top and pulled up the black, well-preserved machine head. Touching her foot to the pedal, she discovered that it worked quite well. This must have belonged to Heath's grandmother. It showed signs of having had loving care.

The drawers of the chest against the wall were empty except for the very bottom one, which contained several thick quilts that smelled sweet from a recent washing. Her troubled blue gaze fell to a sleek modern telephone sitting on the floor by the bed.

She rushed over to it, reciting her sister's number to herself—she would call her sister again and Woody would come and get her out of this mess. But she should have known that no clever kidnapper would install a phone for the convenience of his hostage. The minute she picked up the receiver she heard a ringing buzz, and the finger that jabbed to find a number met only solid plastic. There was no dial on this phone. It was an extension of some sort.

"Hello, Shelby," came Heath's firm masculine voice over the line.

She slammed the receiver down, uttering all kinds of imprecations. Apparently this was a direct line to Heath's office for use in case of emergency.

Clomping across the floor, she stalked out the front door, shoving her hands deep into her jeans pockets in frustration. A dilapidated springhouse sat rakishly over a gurgling narrow stream, and upon investigation Shelby realized that this was her refrigerator, although heaven only knew why she would need it, for all of Montana seemed at this moment to be one vast icebox. The temperature was dropping fast, and poor Shelby's blood chilled in her veins.

There was a shed too, which held stacks of evenly cut lengths of wood and various other paraphernalia that she didn't investigate. A little farther away was another small stout little house with a sloping roof. She opened the door, in which was carved a neat little half moon, and discovered her quite primitive toilet facilities.

Indignant, she marched back into the cabin, picked up the phone receiver and, when Heath answered again, exploded bitterly: "I won't live here. This is sheer madness."

"Tut, tut, my grandparents found the place charmingly comfortable."

"It's uncivilized," she bit back lowly.

"So was my cell in prison," he informed her in an icy tone.

"What kind of a person are you?"

"I've often wondered the same about you."

"Damn!" she whispered helplessly.

"My exact sentiments on many occasions." He harnessed his tones to those of polite courtesy. "I hope you enjoy your stay, my dear."

"Don't you 'my dear' me, you . . . you fiend. If I get mauled by a wild animal out here it will be your fault."

"I'm sure you can deal with any wild animal that comes along," he said mildly, "especially male ones."

She terminated the conversation by crashing the receiver down in its cradle. "Sadistic swine," she fumed, glaring at it impotently.

CHAPTER FOUR

She paced the cabin floor, her thoughts scattered like broken glass. If Heath thought he could reduce her to a babbling, hysterical idiot by thrusting her into this godforsaken hole, he had another thing coming. He was mean and vindictive and made of tempered iron. He would never abandon this diabolical scheme long enough to sit down and listen to her explanation of why she hadn't spoken up for him at the trial—an explanation that certainly couldn't undo the past but might at least make him understand her actions.

She let out a short, exasperated breath and began to cry. He just didn't want to understand—to forgive. And she wasn't about to simper and beg him to. His opinion of her was all too apparent; he thought she was a cheat, a liar, and an immoral woman. Never mind that she had been desperately in love with him. Never mind that her father had threatened her with awful consequences.

Walking to the window, she peered out the dingy glass. Where the hell was she? Which direction was Florida? She'd start off walking right now if she knew the way to go. Turning abruptly, she covered her forehead with a trembling hand. Forcing herself to quit crying, and drying her eyes, she again focused her thoughts on the dismal cabin. For the present, getting it into some kind of habitable condition should be her first priority.

Galvanizing all her energies, she went to the rusty pump and attacked it vigorously. No copious gush issued forth, not even a tiny trickle. It merely creaked and groaned and complained. She cursed it to the very depths of hell, and that didn't help either. Finally, in tears again, she collected a pot from the pantry and traipsed down to the spring for water. It would be just her luck if the lights didn't work either, she fumed. Then she remembered the cabin wasn't wired for electricity and had a few hard moments accepting the fact that her only source of light would be a dusty old lantern.

Back in the cabin she fould some rags, doused them in the frigid water, and began to swab things down without success. She needed soap, better still, carbolic acid. Abandoning this chore as an exercise in futility, she took an old broom, not much more than a stump, and scraped it across the floorboards, managing to capture a few rolls of floating dust and disarrange one or two sticky spider webs.

She slammed the broom on the floor with disgust and stalked toward the door. She liked a place neat! she raved inside. Neat and clean! Apparently her abortive attempts at housekeeping had required so much of her concentration that she had not heard the jeep come up. Heath was leaning against it, his arms folded across his chest, her purse and luggage at his feet. He was perfectly groomed in a pair of dark pants and a white silk shirt, the spotless purity of which fairly enraged her.

"Having trouble, Shelby?" he asked, teeth gleaming through his beard.

"No! Everything is just dandy. I don't have any water, and this place is a pigsty."

"Tsk, tsk," he sympathized.

"You can't tell me you lived in this kind of squalor," she thumbed back toward the cabin, "when you were in prison. The state takes better care of its criminals than that!"

"I wasn't a criminal." He uncrossed his legs and unfolded his arms. He became an angry man of frightening dimensions.

"Well, what you're doing now certainly makes you one," she blazed defensively, "for only a subhuman person would force someone to live in such conditions. I don't even have any drinking water."

His angry expression turned to one of ridicule. "You're so green it makes me laugh." Doing just that, he skirted around her and leaped up the cabin steps. She followed him into the kitchen, eyeing him distrustfully. He rummaged around in a cupboard, finally pulling out a battered old teakettle.

His eyes fell on the tin pot of grimy wash water sitting on the counter. The filthy rag she had used in her efforts to clean floated obscenely on the surface.

"Where did you get that?"

"I fetched it from the spring. And might have caught my death of cold doing it, for that water is just one degree above actual freezing point and it slopped all over me the whole way back."

He threw back his dark saturnine head, and laughter of ridicule boomed from his chest.

"I'm glad you're amused," she said venomously. "And I hope you don't mind paying the hospital bill when I come down with pneumonia."

"I told you there was a well on the back porch."

"So I forgot," she admitted heatedly. "I've never had to

use one before. We don't have much call for them in the city."

"Dumb," he remarked aside. "Dumb, dumb." He took the teakettle out to the back porch, motioning her to follow. She watched him take the plank boards off the well, noting how careful he was not to soil his precious white shirt. The bucket descended into the well with a splash and within moments he had drawn it up and had filled the kettle with fresh, clear water. He carefully replaced the boards and took the kettle back to the kitchen.

"Don't tell me I'm going to have to go through all that every time I want a cup of tea," she scorned.

He held up a hand to silence her. "Observe. Very carefully now," he said with a sarcasm that easily matched hers, "for I have serious misgivings as to your mental capabilities." Rolling up his sleeves and standing well away so as not to spray his immaculate person, he poured the water into the top of the pump and began to work the handle. A bright stream of water rushed from the spout into a crusty old sink. "*Voilà!* This is called priming the pump."

"Amazing!" The corner of her lip lifted in a sneer. "How was I to know that was the way it worked? And what does it solve anyway, if I have to carry in water every time I want to make it go?"

"You only prime it once a day," he explained, fastidiously wiping his fingers on a towel. "My grandmother was ecstatic when Grandfather put it in. In the winter, snow sometimes completely covered the well. With a pump inside she no longer had to fight the drifts and could use melted snow to prime it."

"That's real progress."

He rolled down his sleeves and carefully smoothed out

71

the creases. She noticed the black masculine hairs on his hands as he buttoned his cuffs, and caught the scent of his aftershave.

"Are you going somewhere tonight, or do I assume your impeccable grooming is on my behalf?" She felt decidedly gauche in her red T-shirt and faded jeans.

"I have a dinner date in Butte. Aaron and I will be flying out as soon as I get back to the house, so I just have enough time to deliver your things and go." He checked his wristwatch and frowned.

"Don't let me keep her waiting." Shelby smiled sweetly, ignoring the strange stabbing sensation beneath her breastbone. Why should she care if he had a date? "What's her name? Louise, Frances, Griselda?"

"Christine." He crossed his legs and folded his arms again, assuming an I-don't-give-a-damn attitude. She noticed he did not lean against the sideboard, however, being conscious of its dusty condition. Something in this put her on the very knife edge of uncontrollable rage.

"On your way back from Christine's," she blurted in scathing tones, "how about stopping at a handy discount store and getting me some much needed supplies."

"Besides bringing your clothes, that was precisely my reason for coming out here before taking off," he informed her, keeping the acid in his voice on a level with hers. "What do you need?"

"Dynamite!" she spat.

He shrugged, unfolded his arms, and moved gracefully toward the door.

"Wait!" she called, gulping down her pride.

He turned, smiling satirically, fully aware that he had the upper hand and thoroughly enjoying every minute of it.

You bastard, she accused silently. You arrogant beautiful bastard! "Do you have something to write with?" she asked in a voice barely under control.

He pulled a black leather address book and a gold pen out of his breast pocket.

She smiled wryly. What mundane items were about to be added to his little black book. "Broom, dustpan, mop, cleaning detergent," she began. "Rope."

"Rope?" He looked up, cocking an eyebrow quizzically.

"For a clothesline."

"Okay. Rope."

"A few scatter rugs and some colorful pillows." There was a short, tense silence as he held the pen poised. "Scratch that," she said quickly before he could object. "Just thought I'd ask."

"What else?"

"Material."

"Material?"

"Cloth. Bright prints, vibrant wools. In three-yard lengths or more."

"Really, Shelby," he protested.

"I'm going to make some things for this backwoods ghetto," she informed him defiantly. "Surely you were allowed your little crafts in prison. I understand prisoners do beautiful needlepoint and wood carvings. Well, I want to sew. There's an old machine here and I know how to use it. A prison cell is what you make it, and I intend to make this one as attractive as possible. You can't deny me that," she said huffily, "even if you are a twisted, sadistic monster!"

"Watch your insolent tongue, Shelby. Or I'll shake you until your teeth rattle." Stormy blue locked with obsidian black. He sighed and scribbled on the pad. "Okay, okay. Anything else?"

"Scissors, thread, pins, machine oil." She stopped and bit her lips in embarrassment. "And . . ."

He was still writing. "Yes, go on." He looked up and she shifted uncomfortably. "Is that all?"

"No," she choked. Her hesitation stretched into a lengthy silence.

"Well, what is it you need? Speak now or forever hold your peace."

"Joe Sam and Aaron . . ." she began shakily, ". . . neglected to pack my . . . er . . . underthings."

"I see." He gave a wicked smile and his glittering jet eyes raked over her insinuatingly. "I'll take care of it."

"D-Don't you need to know my sizes?" she stammered.

"I have a very good memory."

She opened her mouth then closed it again as she stifled a groan. Images of that night swept over her with a painful poignancy—that night in his motel room when he had explored every inch of her virgin body and taken it completely as his own possession, that never-to-be-forgotten night when she had become a woman. She strove to keep her emotions under control. "I think I should tell you anyway," she choked. "It would be a shame if you had to fly all the way back to Butte to make exchanges . . . because I wear a very odd size . . ." She stopped, unable to go on.

"Yes?" he urged softly, white flashing through his black-auburn beard.

"Bra!" she exploded. "Thirty-two D."

He gave a low, admiring whistle and her control burst into volcanic eruption. A curse flew out of her mouth at the same time that her hands reached for the nearest object, which happened to be the pot of muddy water on the counter.

For a large man he moved quickly, and the noxious liquid barely spattered his black lizard-hide shoes. As the empty pot came to a clattering halt on the floor, acquiring several new dents in the process, her temper spent itself. The black haze of anger lifted from her vision and his face became distinct. The expression she saw on it struck fear in her heart.

He advanced on her inexorably and her eyes widened with apprehension. When he came within an arm's length, she lashed out helplessly.

"Don't you try to hit me on top of everything else, you little hellcat." He had intercepted her arm and held it in a manacle of iron; he could have snapped it as easily as a toothpick.

"Take your filthy paws off me!"

This final defiance broke every pretense of civility. He pulled her into his body as a tender wild thing crushed against a wall of granite. When she tried to claw his face, he captured the free arm and forced it behind her back. Then he pulled her up and forward, molding her to his hard hips.

"Now what are you going to do?" he asked softly, menacingly.

"Let me go!" she ordered breathlessly.

His teeth showed and the next moment they were biting her lips. She pulled her head back but he followed her relentlessly, his attack becoming a wide, savage kiss that drained the sweetness from her mouth and probed every tender recess. He held her wrists in one hand and allowed the other to run over her body at will, cupping her breast with rough caresses and seizing intimate places with furious expertise.

His mouth was fierce and hurting and his violent fondlings were without respect. She cried inwardly and must have made a pathetic sound deep in her soul, for all of a sudden he released her and stood back breathing heavily. One hand trembled to her bruised lips and the other to her aching breasts. A dozen scathing remarks came to her mind, but she clamped her teeth against saying any of them, knowing she could not withstand any more of this kind of punishment.

Apparently he didn't trust himself to speak either. He compressed his lips and turned on his heels abruptly. Within moments she heard the grinding of gears and the sound of the jeep speeding across the prairie.

Deeply offended, she shambled into the living room and out the front door, collapsing on the rickety front steps in a posture of dejection.

She sat there alone for what seemed like an eternity but must have only been moments. The intensely chilly wind invaded the bare flesh of her arms and penetrated her thin shirt until discomfort made her rise stiffly to fetch her smart leather luggage, which sat incongruously in its wilderness surroundings where Heath had abandoned it.

She carried the luggage to the bedroom and slowly and methodically unpacked her belongings, refolding them and stacking them neatly in the dresser drawers.

That done, she wandered to the pantry and rummaged around among the tinned goods and packages. Gray shadows of evening invaded the cabin. It was suppertime but she had no appetite. Even if she had, the cast-iron wood stove posed problems too overwhelming for her benumbed brain to deal with at the present time. She wasn't a pioneer woman and had never been a Girl Scout.

She opened a pack of saltines, ate two mechanically, then tossed the rest back on the shelf. Thirsty now, she went into the kitchen and pumped some water into a dented tin cup that looked clean enough. The water had a taste of iron. She made a face and threw the remains, together with the cup, into the sink.

The sharp noise of its impact startled her. Suddenly she was aware of the profound silence surrounding her. Never before had she experienced such stillness. It was as if she were all alone in the middle of the universe. There were no muted traffic sounds in the distance, no muffled doors slamming from nearby dwelling places, no faint echoes of human speech and children's laughter. Even the comfortable hum of a refrigerator was denied her as she stood in the cold dead silence of her wilderness prison and watched the shadows of night creep inexorably closer and closer.

She decided she must build a fire in the fireplace. She collected a copious supply of wood from the woodshed and paper and matches from the pantry. The paper burned but the logs would not catch.

Successfully building this fire became the focal point of her existence. She imagined it to be the very essence of survival and understood now why primitive man had been goaded into discovering it. Her need for its warmth and friendliness and light had become a deep hunger.

Patiently and painstakingly, she rearranged the logs and sticks to allow for more air circulation. At last the flames from the burning paper rolled around the wood, penetrated it, and began to feed and grow.

She sat back on her aching haunches and silently welcomed this only friend and companion to share her dismal existence. It crackled and snapped a cheerful greeting as night closed off the gray light of evening like a black curtain.

She rose and walked to the naked windows to peer out. This Montana night was absolute. There were no streetlights, no yellow porch lights—not even a moon or a few brave little stars.

She turned away shuddering and trying to hold in abeyance her conflicting emotions and her growing fear. The fire illuminated the living room, and its glowing light filtered into the kitchen and bedroom. Shelby drew some water into a bowl and found a clean rag in one of the cupboard drawers. Without undressing, she stood by the sink and gave herself a quick washup, trying to ignore the huge grotesque shadows her own body threw on the walls.

She knew she must make a trip to the outhouse before finally dressing for bed and pondered the problem in all its intricacies, as one preparing to climb Mount Everest or swim the English Channel.

Finally working out what she hoped was a sound plan of action, she put on her short coat and went to the table to study the lantern. After experimenting for a few seconds she discovered that the chimney lifted off to expose the wick. The bottom globe of the lantern was full of a liquid she assumed must be coal oil, and despite her ignorance of such matters, she reasoned the protruding wick would have absorbed enough fuel to catch a flame.

She was right. The wick stole the fire of her match with ease. She carefully replaced the glass chimney, propped the cabin door open with the butter churn to let out more light, and walked out onto the front porch.

Black, unearthly silence closed in on her. In Florida one could always hear the chirp of crickets. She could only suppose that here they were too cold to rub their stiff little legs together.

It was as if she were on the edge of outer space. She went back into the cabin and clasped two trembling hands around the bowl of the lantern, holding it before her face like a candle-bearing nun on her way to vespers.

She and her pitiful pool of light moved slowly toward the outhouse. Cold fingers of fear wrapped around her throat and blocked off her breathing. Her ears strained for sounds. A grizzly bear might loom down on her at any moment, or the legendary sasquatch. She peered at the ground; there could be snakes. She squinted into the darkness for the glowing eyes of wild things that could lunge and bite—coyotes, wolves.

Her fear grew, and she teetered on the edge of panic. A helpless cry caught in her throat. She was alone, alone in this awful darkness. And the man who had put her here was gorging himself in Butte with warmth and food and that tender morsel named Christine.

Anger mingled with fear and gave her strength. At last she found the wooden door with the half-moon-shaped hole in it. Out of anger and sheer madcap audacity she hit the door with her fist. If there were any creatures inside, she would scare them away: offense was the best defense.

The door creaked as she inched it open. Once within its crude cobwebbed confines, a new wave of anger engulfed her. "Damn you, Heath Tanner! Damn! Damn!"

She didn't like exposing her tenderest parts to a drafty unknown.

She didn't linger, but cursed Heath repeatedly while scrambling to zip her jeans. Grabbing her lantern, she pushed her way out and made haste toward the open cabin door and the friendly firelight.

As she clamored up the steps she heard a horrifying screech overhead and the flapping of wings.

"Oh my God!" She darted through the door like a vibrating arrow, slammed it shut, and shot the bolt. Only then did she let herself set the lantern on the table and crumple on the crude bench beside it.

It was an owl, she reasoned. Some kind of bird. A helpless sob tore from her throat, and she clenched her fists to her head. "You're not going to get away with this, Heath," she vowed. "I'll find a way out. You can bet your sweet life on it."

Through the oppressive silence she heard a distinct rattling sound. Her blood froze, and her tears turned into the moisture of fear. It was coming from the pantry. She stumbled silently to her feet and plastered herself against the wall. There was something or someone in the pantry. She was caught between two hells—something menacing and unknown in the pantry or the great engulfing darkness outside. Should she stay or run? The choices were impossible.

Paralyzed, she stared at the pantry door, her eyes enormous. The rattling continued. A vapor of terror filled her throat and erupted in a strangled scream. As if in response, there was more activity in the pantry. The door opened slightly and a dark shape scuttled across the room.

Shelby yelped and jumped up on the bench. At first she thought it was a gigantic rat. But as it ran toward her she saw its mask and ringed tail. "Get out of here!" she screamed.

The raccoon veered to the left in a frantic effort to do just that. He bumped into the closed door in his panic, and Shelby was faced with the problem of helping him escape. Raccoons being curious by nature, he had apparently wandered through the open door while she was out, investigated the pantry, and found the open pack of saltines.

Shelby jumped from the bench and unbolted and opened the door in a flash, peeking around the edge to see what the disoriented animal would do. Scenting the night air, he waddled through the door, undoubtedly as relieved to be rid of Shelby as she was of him.

In the aftermath of this crisis, Shelby broke down completely and gave in to squalling hysteria. She cried until her face puffed up and she was too tired to produce any more tears.

Her eyes burned and her head throbbed well into the night, and even a cold compress didn't assuage the pain that tension, fear, and anger had brought on.

She didn't fall asleep until a rosy dawn bled into the eastern sky. And her last thought before dropping off was of escape.

CHAPTER FIVE

She was sitting on the stoop of her little postage-stamp-size front porch shivering in the brisk noonday wind when Joe Sam pulled up in the Scout. Shelby gave him a baleful look as he walked up the front steps and deposited a box of fresh produce and wrapped meat beside her.

"There's a week's supply here," he said gruffly. "It will keep well in the springhouse this time of year." His keen black eyes examined her closely, and he became quiet and thoughtful.

"Thanks," she said shortly, turning her face away to hide the telltale signs of what she had gone through the night before.

Joe Sam didn't answer. Only a slight tightening of his immobile features belied his concern.

He lit a pipe, seeming in no particular hurry to leave. She was grudgingly thankful. Even his company was preferable to being alone. She was already dreading another night by herself in the cabin.

"Where exactly am I, if you don't mind my asking?"

"Planning escape?" He didn't actually chuckle, but she fancied there was one lurking somewhere beneath his calm exterior.

"Would it do me any good?"

"No. You'd never make it out of this wilderness on foot."

"I figured that. Where are we anyway? Just for the sake of conversation."

"You are on a large spread south of the Blackfoot Indian Reservation, not far from the Lewis Upthrust, which forms the continental divide this side of Glacier National Park."

"I see," she said, not really comprehending at all.

The merest hint of a smile pulled at the corner of his mouth. "You are in northwestern Montana," he explained, "majestic climbing Rockies on one side, vast rolling prairie on the other—the best possible place on earth to be. Over there," he pointed through the trees to the purple-hazed mountains, "rises the continental divide, North America's backbone, where streams flow west into the Pacific on one side and east to the Mississippi on the other. On farther up north there is a mountain called Triple Divide Peak from which streams flow not only east and west, but north too, to Hudson Bay."

"It's very different here from what I'm used to. Beautiful, but a little too chilly for my comfort."

"You're a Southern girl," he observed. "White Brave's mother was too."

"Heath's mother was from the South?" Shelby asked with interest.

"Her family moved here from Louisiana. She was of a delicate constitution. One winter she caught pneumonia and never recovered. Heath's father, my son, was killed in a hunting accident the next autumn."

"Oh," she breathed, "I'm sorry."

He looked away to the mountains. "What have you eaten?"

"Crackers and peanut butter." She got up suddenly and with energetic nonchalance, intending to prove she didn't require his concern or any subsequent pity. She bent to lift the box, but he whisked it out from under her nose and carried it into the cabin.

"I'll teach you how to operate the stove," he said ceremonially.

"Why don't you just take me out of this hellhole?" she shot back in helpless anger.

"That would solve nothing."

"That would solve everything!"

He ignored this outburst and stolidly motioned her to the stove. Patiently, he meticulously described every step toward arousing the black-legged antique to vibrant roaring heat. Soon perking coffee was sending out its own fragrant aroma and bacon and eggs were sizzling and popping in a pan.

Surprisingly, Shelby discovered the old Indian was an easy person to be around. He was undemanding and restful in his manners and not at all the brute she had thought he was at first. She could probably take to him if it weren't for the fact that he had plotted this horrendous abduction.

In his calm, implacable way he made her sit down and eat the hot food while he had his pipe and coffee. She didn't argue since the smell of the cooking had made her almost faint with hunger. When she was full at last, she cradled her mug between two white hands and looked at him across the table.

"Thank you for showing me how to use the stove," she said politely. "You are a good teacher in the art of survival."

"An Indian has to be." He placed his cup on the table and quietly nursed his pipe. "I taught White Brave everything he knows about ranching, hunting, fending for himself. We had many good times together before he left for college, then went about the country on his nomadic search for experiences." The cold afternoon sun burnished his coppery skin. "I wish to God he'd never left Montana. He would never have gotten into trouble here as he did in so-called civilization."

Shelby's thick smoky lashes swept her cheeks and she took a sip of coffee. "Why do you call him White Brave?" she asked, maneuvering around the painful subject of Heath's imprisonment.

"It's the Indian name I gave him when he saved my life."

"Heath saved your life? You're kidding."

He leveled her a look silently stating that he never kidded. "It happened many years ago," he said, "when my grandson was just a boy. About twelve or so, as I recall." His eyes misted. "It was autumn, about this time of the year. I had promised him a real hunting trip, deep into the woods. Even at that age he could handle a gun like a seasoned hunter. I knew the route of the birds' flyway, as we call it, and my young grandson was keen to shoot his first geese. The first day we got nine. We cleaned them near our camp, then hung them up, as it was cool and they would keep. We ate supper of prairie chicken roasted over an open fire. Then I watched my grandson drift off into a deep peaceful sleep.

"The next morning a foot of snow lay on the ground. We shot about two dozen birds that morning, and we went out and got that many more in the afternoon. I told my grandson we had gotten enough, for I was concerned that a big snow would come upon us. My grandson was disappointed when we broke camp the next morning, but I reasoned with him that his grandmother's fiery temper would be aroused if we brought home too much meat for her to can and smoke."

"Was it on the way home that Heath saved your life?" Shelby probed curiously.

"Yes. I went on ahead to do a little more hunting on my own, feeling confident that my grandson knew enough to take care of himself. I had taught him to watch his back carefully." The old Indian paused. "But that day it was old Joe Sam who made mistakes. I did not wait to study the woods. I walked too fast. I should have read the signs of danger before walking straight into the bush and thicket. I surprised the Sim-a-hi. She was lying half asleep by an old rotten log."

"Sim-a-hi?"

"Grizzly bear," he translated.

She shuddered. "What did you do?"

"I made another mistake. I shot too quick. The grizzly is very bad medicine. One has to shoot true. I didn't do that. She turned on me mad, very mad. I backed away. She charged me, her mouth frothing insanely. I emptied my rifle into her. She still came. Suddenly my grandson shot from out of nowhere, two well-aimed bullets straight into the base of her neck. She fell like a great tree right at my feet—dead."

"My Lord," Shelby breathed.

"I cut off her front claw," he went on, "and made a hero's necklace out of it for my grandson. In the very old days, when the plains were thick with great herds of buffalo and every kind of wildlife, it was the greatest honor for an Indian warrior to shoot the Sim-a-hi. Many went through life never achieving this distinction, for the Sim-a-hi is powerfully mean, a great killer. And my grandson, only a child, showed much bravery. So I have called him White Brave from that day to this." He got up and moved to the window to look out.

Shelby stared into her empty cup, remembering. "Yes, Heath is an exceptional man," she admitted softly.

"Such a man should have many sons." The old man's voice was heavy with sadness.

"Oh, Heath will get married. I'm surprised he hasn't already." In the past, during moments of deep psychological pain, she had wished him happily married. "I wish him well; I always have. But it shocks me to see him so bitter and hateful."

"White Brave is a man haunted by the past," Joe Sam remarked. He nodded toward the somber, purple-swathed mountains in the distance. "His emotions are as timeless and primitive as the earth itself. They have stolen his joy ... and perhaps his ability to love. Deeply, as a man needs to love."

"Are you saying that Heath is not capable of falling in love?"

Joe Sam shrugged, refusing to comment further concerning his grandson. "I must go now. Dove will worry. Lock your door after I leave. Never take anything for granted in the wilderness."

"I guess I can handle myself," she said with bravado, her chin tilting defiantly.

He glanced at her. "Yes, it seems you can. I knew you were an unusual woman when I stuck my knife to your throat and you gave me back that blue stony stare of courage. An Indian always admires courage."

Shelby wondered how brave he would have thought she was if he'd seen her last night. "Why did you do it, Joe Sam?" she suddenly blurted out. "Why did you come up

87

with this awful kidnapping idea? Heath told me you suggested it. Why? Why?"

"Because I knew something had to be done. I thought if I brought you face to face with him he would be able to sort out his feelings. I even half hoped he would take one look at you after so long and send you away, wondering why on earth he had allowed you to get such a hold on him. That was a foolish hope. I see now that you are the kind of woman who could drive a man insane."

"You don't see anything!" she exploded. "You don't know me at all. You know nothing about what I am really like or what I feel."

"I know you have terrible nightmares of White Brave." He put his hand on the doorknob. "That was very enlightening. Your guilt, his hate—an interesting combination." He opened the door and exited before she could think of a suitable retort.

It took nearly the entire afternoon to scrub the cooking utensils they had used and stow the perishables in the springhouse. She washed her only set of lingerie and hung it over the edge of the table, then decided there was nothing else to be done inside the cabin without the supplies Heath would be bringing her. So she buttoned on her suede jacket and struck off down a rocky path with the intention of becoming more familiar with her surroundings and perhaps finding a way of escape.

A little distance away she discovered a wide glassy lake that reflected the cloudless sky in deep blue. There was a strange rock nearby, shaped like a huge grotesque teapot. She climbed upon it and settled herself listlessly. Perhaps Joe Sam was right. Perhaps there was no way out of this wilderness on foot. Loneliness and resentment engulfed her, touched by shades of something else she couldn't define—something very much like grief.

Dreaded evening stole in and muted the landscape around her like a gray silent predator. With a deep sigh she slid from the rock and made her way back to the cabin. Her supper was canned beef stew warmed on the stove, which, once mastered, was proving simple enough to operate but dreadfully time consuming.

She made her trip to the outhouse before night descended in earnest, then gave her face and hands a good scrubbing, using the creaky pump and a shallow pan. How in the world had Heath's grandmother, paragon that she was, ever managed to get a full bath or wash her hair, she wondered.

After locking the door, she blew out the lantern, pushed the coals of the fire well to the back of the fireplace, and climbed into the clean, fresh bed, knowing sleep would be impossible.

Her thoughts turned reluctantly to the enigmatic Joe Sam. She felt both angered and awed by him. He obviously had brought her here so that Heath could play some cat-and-mouse game—so that he could toy with her mercilessly until boredom set in and he turned her loose. But Shelby was no meek little mouse. She had no intentions of allowing Heath to bully her, destroy her. Joe Sam had not brought Heath a mouse at all, but a cat—one who could unsheathe her claws when necessary. Apparently he realized this now and had decided it was going to be interesting to stand back and watch the fur fly.

How much more civilized it would be if she and Heath could just sit down and talk it all out amicably. She would explain everything. He would understand, perhaps forgive. He might even come to the point of regarding her with a little friendliness. But no, talking with him rationally was impossible. The tension in the air when they were together was alive with something much more complex than simple hatred. Joe Sam had said it was as primitive as the nearby mountains dominating this Montana countryside.

She shifted in the bed restlessly. She would never get to sleep with all these disturbing thoughts in her mind and surrounded by this filthy environment. But, as a gift of mercy, exhaustion took over and submerged her into a deep, dream-haunted slumber.

At about two o'clock in the morning she woke up in a violent sweat. The cabin was completely dark except for the feeble glow cast by the dying embers in the fireplace. In the past when these horrible nightmares had gripped her she had always looked to Luann for comfort. Even after moving into the city of Orlando, she had called her sister many times in the middle of the night, and her sister, muzzy from sleep, would talk about anything and everything until the horror had dissipated.

Automatic reflex made her grab for the telephone. Immediately, Heath's groggy voice came over the line, "What is it, Shelby? Are you all right?"

"Oh no," she moaned as a mortal confronted suddenly by a ghost. Dropping the receiver back into its cradle, she turned her face into the pillow and strove to subdue the trembling of her body. After a few minutes she eased off the bed, still in the grip of total and unreasonable fear. She was fumbling for the teakettle when the lights of the jeep danced in the window, catching her and pinning her in suspended animation like a paralyzed rabbit. Dazed with the unreality of her surroundings and the aftermath of the nightmare, she crouched back and shrank into a corner.

"Shelby!" Heath rattled the doorknob. "Let me in!"

A comic hysteria swamped her as she recalled the story of the three little pigs and the big bad wolf.

"Go away!" she screamed.

Suddenly one of the windows slammed up explosively and Heath was levering himself into the cabin.

"Get away!" she quavered. "Don't come near me."

In two long strides he had her against his chest, running his hands down her arms and turning them over to check her wrists. She sank against him like a rag doll, listening to the thundering of his heart in her ear.

"Oh, Shell, what have you done to yourself?" he asked in a voice husky with fear. Putting his hands to the sides of her face, he lifted it for inspection. It was pale, overwhelmed with enormous, uncomprehending eyes. "Tell me you haven't hurt yourself. Tell me you're all right."

"I'm all right," she said through pinched, dry lips.

He pulled her to his chest again and she realized it was bare. He had not taken time to put on a shirt or button the jacket he'd thrown on in his haste to get to her. She nuzzled into his chest hair and drew from his warmth. With its inflowing came a sense of reality and the knowledge of where she was and what had happened.

Softly he stroked her head. "What scared you?" he murmured. "You look as if you've seen a ghost."

This was heaven, being held in his arms. Secretly she brushed her lips across his salty-sweet skin. Her arms stole around his back and hugged him close. Warm blood stole into her limbs and rushed to heat her blanched face. She felt his lips in her hair and wanted to die. She had seen her ghost. And now she was holding him. The nightmare was gone, but she still held her dream.

91

"Tell me," he said against her forehead. "Tell me what frightened you so."

"It was a nightmare," she whimpered softly.

He pushed her away and held her at arm's length. "A nightmare? You scared the hell out of me over some silly nightmare?" Giving her a little shove, he turned abruptly and stalked around the cabin like an angry animal, running his fingers through his hair and rubbing the back of his neck. "A nightmare!" he exploded. "And I thought you had . . ."

"Slit my wrists?" she challenged. "Do you think I have a reason to do that? When you thought I had, did you feel any pain or remorse? Or were you happy? Sorry I woke you for nothing, Heath. Next time I'll make it worth your while." Vaguely she registered the fact that they couldn't be in a room together two minutes without engaging in clawing combat. Something about that made her ache with sadness.

"Just don't cry wolf like this again," he warned, stopping in front of her and sticking his finger under her nose.

"Oh, I won't. Or the wolf might come running."

"Don't bait me, Shelby. I'm angry and I'm very tired."

"What's the matter? Did Christine wear you out?"

"No, she didn't wear me out. She was all pleasantness, much different from you."

"I'll bet!" Pain slashed across her chest, and she refused to believe it was jealousy.

His hand clamped around her upper arm and drew her forward. "Just remember not to call me again . . . for nothing."

Nothing! He was saying her nightmares were nothing! "Haven't you ever had a horrible dream?" she asked spittingly. "Are you quite human?"

"Yes, I had my share of them. In prison. But I never called my warden moaning like a banshee, expecting him to come hold my hand."

"I didn't ask you to come out here. I was half asleep and thought I was calling Luann. She always helped me out of these bad times."

His grip on her arm softened. "Then you've had these nightmares before?" he asked with a puzzled frown.

"For the past seven years," she whispered. "And it's one dream that keeps recurring over and over. The trial—that awful trial."

Slowly he released her. They stood staring at each other, their eyes deep with pain and a million conflicting emotions.

"Fix yourself some tea," he said curtly, turning to leave. "Then go back to bed. And learn to handle your nightmares by yourself; I have enough of my own to worry about."

After he was gone, she fumbled around in the pantry for the tea bags, unable to see them through blinding tears. "You're all heart, Mr. Tanner, all heart."

With a tremulous sigh she began the tedious procedure of building a fire in the stove and preparing the teakettle. After an inordinate amount of time and effort, she had her little cup of tea. Every sip of the amber liquid further calmed her and infused her with a renewed determination to free herself of Heath Tanner.

Perhaps she could hike the distance to the house, steal the keys to the Scout, and escape to the nearest town. She set the cup on the dusty table and shook her head. That wouldn't work. Down deep, she knew she could never pull it off. In the first place, approaching the house unseen by Dove, Joe Sam, or Heath seemed highly unlikely. And even if she could manage to gain entrance to the house, where would she look for the Scout keys? In Heath's pocket? She gave a rueful laugh, rose from the table, and took her cup to the sink. And supposing that by some miraculous series of events she did manage to get access to the jeep. Where would she go? She had no idea of the direction to the nearest town—Choteau, was it? And there were no friendly pedestrians strolling about to offer advice and assistance. She could take a wrong road and wind up deeper in the wilderness than she was at the present time, lost, alone, and even more at the mercy of the elements.

No. Trying to steal Heath's jeep was a bad idea. There had to be a better way. But she was too tired and muddled to think of it now. She scuffled into the bedroom and got back into bed. More than anything she wanted to see and talk with her sister, Luann. She knew if she could get to a telephone she could call Luann, explain everything, and Woody would come after her. Not only would Woody come after her, but he would undoubtedly be in a rage, for he was very protective where family was concerned. He and Heath might actually come to blows. The police might get involved. It could result in a reenactment of the past. Too painful even to contemplate.

Her mind recoiled at the thought of involving Luann and Woody in this. They were happy and content running their citrus grove on the outskirts of Orlando and raising their two kids. She would not let Heath Tanner turn their lives upside down too. Her sister was under the impression that she was out here rekindling her old romance with Heath. She would allow her sister to continue with that illusion. Shelby would find her own way out, without disturbing her sister's world.

The next day about midmorning Heath drove up in the

jeep. She was inside the cabin finishing up what few chores she could without the supplies she so badly needed. He opened the door without knocking and stepped inside—a huge, wide figure that dominated the tiny cabin with its presence. Sunlight bathed his dark head, sparking the auburn threads to fiery brilliance.

"I brought your supplies."

"Thanks." She turned to her dishes and attacked them with a tea towel.

Slowly he devoured every curve of her body, the wide, shapely hips, the Scarlett O'Hara waist, the jutting breasts, free of the confines of a bra, swaying tantalizingly as she moved to put the dishes on the shelf.

She had an exceptional body. Any man with less than adequate vision could see that. And Heath's eyes were keen, the eyes of a hunter. She didn't hear the ragged breath escape from his chest, nor did she see the torment in his eyes as he forced himself to turn away.

She adopted an attitude of mild curiosity as he unloaded box after box from the jeep. Soon half the floor of the living room was covered.

"There's more here than you asked for," he said, "but I'm sure you'll need it all."

"I appreciate that." Hands on hips, she moved among the supplies with lazy disinterest. "I'm glad you thought of shampoo," she remarked, touching one of the boxes with her toe. "But how does one go about washing her hair out here, if you don't mind a stupid question. Wait for it to rain?"

His biceps bulged as he set the last carton on the floor. "You might say that." He straightened, folded his arms over his massive chest, and gave her a twisted smile.

95

"Grandma used the rain barrel, at least during those months it wasn't frozen solid."

"Rain barrel?" she echoed stupidly.

"There's one out back. Just pull the stopper, and you'll have a continuous stream of water that should last through two soapings."

"How convenient. I've never had the luxury of washing my hair with ice water."

Wry amusement pulled at the corner of his mouth. "Yes, I'm afraid it will be quite cold," he agreed. "Of course, I never had to use it; we had a hot water heater in the frame house where my foreman now lives. But Grandma frequently commented on how cold it was. Said it would knock a person's eyes out."

"Oh, terrific!"

Heath lounged against the table, biting the inside of his cheek to keep from laughing. "Yes, Grandma swore by her rainwater," he went on wickedly. "Said it cleared the cobwebs out of the brain."

"I can imagine!"

"After she and Grandfather moved in with us, she rode over here every week just to wash her hair."

"She must have been a masochist."

White teeth showed through the glinting beard. "Not really. It was sheer vanity that sent her over here every Saturday morning. The rainwater made her hair silky and fragrant. And Grandma was very proud of her head of long fiery red hair."

A lightbulb flashed in Shelby's brain. "How far did she have to ride? The foreman's house must be pretty close-by."

He laughed soundlessly, catching immediately the turn of her thoughts. "Our old house, which is now my foreman's house, is seven miles away," he provided easily. "Seven miles of rough country teeming with big cats, grizzly bears, and snakes of every description. Grandma was a seasoned backwoods woman. She rode over on horseback, and more important, she had a gun and knew how to use it."

She could tell by his wide grin that he was exaggerating. Surely there weren't that many wild animals or . . . ugh . . . snakes. But then it would take just one encounter with a wild cat, wouldn't it? The result of just one tangle would be absolute and final. Her brain revolved in sluggish uncertainty. And what would she tell the foreman once she got there, if she did? That his boss was a kidnapper and a sadistic beast? Would he believe it, or would he think she was a raving lunatic?

"Stick close to the cabin, Shelby," Heath warned her, all vestiges of his grin now gone. "You're too inexperienced; you could get hurt."

"Isn't that what you want?" she spat venomously. "To see me hurt? Wouldn't it do your evil heart—and I use the word heart for lack of a better term—good to see me lying dead somewhere, mangled and bleeding from a fall or some large animal? Wouldn't that satisfy, like nothing else, your diabolical desire for revenge?"

He lunged forward and grasped her by the shoulders. "Shut up!"

"What are you going to do now?" She was in a vibrating rage. "Bruise me again with your hands, like you did the other day? Go ahead, ease your hate, Heath. Ease your hate by hurting me."

His hand closed over her mouth and stopped her words. They stared into one another's eyes and became very still. Slowly his hand moved from her mouth to caress the side of her face. His head bent and his lips took hers softly, applying gentle pressure as if he were tasting, savoring, remembering. His tongue explored the inside parts of her lips, then probed farther, capturing, lingering in the deepest and sweetest recesses of her mouth.

For a moment she was lost. This was Heath. Her lover. She offered no resistance as he pulled her hips forward, molding her to his passion, pressing her against him with a tender hunger.

"I never forgot you, Shell." His sensuous lips had broken with hers and were now moving against the tender flesh of her neck. "Your scent—tantalizing, delicate, sweet." He crushed her soft voluptuous breasts against his chest. "Do you remember that night in my room? That night when I made you mine completely?"

She gave a soft, helpless moan. "What do you want from me, Heath?"

"I don't know." He raised his head and his beard grazed her cheek. "I don't know what I want from you. Let's experiment."

"No!" She began to struggle. "I won't play this kind of game with you!"

He silenced her with his mouth, not savagely or tenderly, but with an intent that was purely sexual. His hand touched her breast intimately, circling her taut nipple with his gentle fingers and with expertise. Her eyes flew open as a shock of flaming desire ripped through her midsection.

"How many have there been since me, Shelby?" His fiery breath fanned her pulsating lips. "I nearly went crazy thinking about that in prison. How many men have enjoyed what you gave me first?"

Her hands came against him in tight fists, and she

shoved him violently. "Dozens!" she spat angrily. "I didn't bother to count them all."

He released her and she stumbled over to the table, grabbing it for support.

His eyes glittered like hard black diamonds. "I think I can cope with that. The fact that you're a little shopworn won't keep me from having a satisfying relationship with you."

"You're out of your mind," she breathed in horror.

"Think about it," he urged suggestively. "I'll be back later."

Only after the jeep had roared off over the prairie did she back away from the table and shamble over to the boxes of supplies. Shock, anger, and humiliation revolved inside her and sickened her stomach. Was there no end to this man's effrontery? First he kidnaps her and thrusts her in these uninhabitable surroundings, then he has the audacity to suggest she become his own personal usable commodity.

No way! No way would she allow him to use her in this manner. If he tried, he would soon realize he had finally met up with a wildcat in the wilderness. Let him think what he liked about "other men"—he was bound and determined to anyway.

She dived into the boxes with an angry determination that had nothing to do with unpacking the supplies. What she found further confirmed the direction Heath's thinking had taken.

There was a tub of all sorts of cleaning paraphernalia and a wooden box containing sweets and various tins and packages of good things to eat, including imported Swedish cookies and spiced tea from England. A box of sewing supplies passed her inspection as well as a leather book of stationery. He had conceded and bought a rug and some expensive velvet pillows. All these things were innocuous enough. It was the other things that bothered her and compounded her anger.

There were boxes and boxes of clothing—soft cowl-neck sweaters, wool ski pants with little loops that fit under the feet, two pairs of very costly fleece-lined boots, a beautiful fire-engine-red parka lined with cream-colored fleece, a long, elegant cobalt-blue robe, a pair of blue woolly-looking boot-shaped slippers to match. Finally there was a box of the requested underclothing. Instead of these being the practical cotton variety she had expected, they were sheer bits of black and beige nylon, trimmed with the most gorgeous silks and laces.

Price tags still hung from everything, blatant pendants of how very, very expensive these things had been. The coat alone had cost what it took her a week to earn. The price of one of the sweaters was so out of sight that she was afraid to lift it out of the box, much less wear it.

Shelby knew that Heath had bought her these outrageously costly and lovely items with one thing in mind—what he could get in return. His intentions were coming through loud and clear; she would have to make hers louder and clearer.

As a diversionary measure, and to preserve what little sanity she had left, Shelby dived into cleaning the front room. With the energy of a tigress she scrubbed and scoured until one could have eaten off the old plank floor. She washed down the furniture, scraped the old stove, and swept out the fireplace, even attacking its outside bricks with a stiff sudsy brush.

She would find the foreman's house as soon as possible. There must be some kind of trail. So much for Heath's trying to scare her away with tales of vicious animals and rattlesnakes. If his grandmother could make the trip, so could she. She didn't need a horse. She was young and healthy and seven miles wasn't such a very long way to walk.

After cleaning the cabin, she suffered the rain barrel, cursing Heath for every quick indrawn breath it took to withstand it. Then she laid a fire in the fireplace and sat down to dry her hair. Heath's grandmother had been right. It did clear the cobwebs. She felt alert and restless—alive and longing for people, their loud voices and laughter.

She built a fire in the stove, ate a bite, and put on some water for her bath. She would have a proper one tonight in the new metal tub Heath had brought.

When it was half full of hot water, she dragged it over before the fireplace. Before beginning to undress, she put some of the new material over the curtain rods to ensure privacy. Even though there was no one around for miles, the idea of bathing in front of unadorned windows was unappealing.

The bath was soothing, and after soaping her body into a rich lather while standing, she contorted her limbs into a sitting position and stayed there like a mesmerized pretzel. She wondered if Heath would show up to torment her tonight. He had said that he would see her later. That could mean tonight or next year; the man was as predictable as a cobra. She marshaled her defenses and set her jaw in a line of stubborn determination.

The water was now tepid. She got out, wrapped in one of the new plush towels Heath had bought her, and scooted the tub into a corner to be emptied in the morning. Shivering, she went into the bedroom and put on her warmest nightgown, glancing longingly at the new satin robe folded neatly in a bed of tissue paper.

It looked warm and so elegant with its oriental embroidery. She gave in and tried it on. Blue was one of her best colors, making her hair as black as a raven's wing and her eyes as deep as lake water reflecting a cloudless sky. She decided to keep the robe and matching bootlike slippers but nothing else. The rest of the clothing would have to be sent back for less expensive things—things she could afford to pay for herself with the last month's wages Mr. Tate would certainly be sending her soon. She was no fool; she realized the necessity of winter clothing here in Montana, but nothing so outrageously expensive. And not at the price Heath expected for payment!

Although out in the middle of nowhere, she wore makeup every day, done lightly but perfectly. Then at night she meticulously cleaned it off, just as if everything were normal and she were still leading her full, well-ordered life back in Orlando. After making sure that the satiny skin on her face was smooth and free of everything except a little shine left from her scented cleansing cream, she hugged the flowing sleeves of the robe and padded back to sit in front of the fire, feeling the deepest wave of loneliness she had yet endured.

Unhappily she stared at the flames, wishing fervently she would keel over from exhaustion and fall into a deep, mindless sleep.

CHAPTER SIX

Heath's knock roused her from her deep broodings. Realizing it would be futile to try to keep him out, she slowly got up and opened the door. He pushed his way inside as she retreated to the braided rug in front of the fire.

"Is the warden doing his nightly rounds?" she asked caustically. "Or do you consider yourself more than a warden since buying me all those beautiful clothes in there?" She tossed her head, indicating the bedroom.

"You're very quick." He unbuttoned his suede fleece-lined coat and threw it on the table. "It must come from your extensive experience in these matters."

He walked over, completely engulfing her with his male presence, bringing with him the fresh night air and an aroma all his own. "Well, aren't you going to invite me to sit down and share your fire?"

Her first instinct was to scream no and order him out, but she knew that would be fruitless. She spread her arm in a wide arc over the thick braided rug in mute, sarcastic invitation.

He sat down, leaned against one of the pillows, and brooded over her with black, dangerous eyes. He reached out and fingered the lace-ruffled sleeve of the robe. "It suits you, rich and exotic, soft and alluring."

Her chin tilted to an angle of defiance. "I'll accept it on the condition that I pay you back when Mr. Tate sends me my last month's wages. The other things must be returned."

"Not necessary," he said easily. "Keep everything. You're my prisoner and I intend to keep you in style."

"I have no intention of being a kept woman, Heath," she informed him in a low, steady voice.

"Why not? We're both adults. You're no longer the inexperienced, overconfident child you were at seventeen. You're a woman now—a woman who has been around. You've had many admirers. Why not add me to the list?" His rough hand reached under the blue satin sleeve and caressed her arm persuasively.

She jerked it away. "I don't understand you at all. How can you even be suggesting this? I'm not at all what you think I am. And besides, you hate me. How can you hate me and want me at the same time? It's . . . it's bizarre!"

"That's true," he agreed with sardonic humor. "I've suffered the two opposing emotions for seven years. I want you as a man in the desert wants a drink of water, yet at times I find you as unwelcome to my thoughts as death." He pulled her down beside him confidently. "But right now I'm hungering and thirsting for you." His lips began their descent. "Give me a drink, Shell."

"You're crazy!" She wrenched free and lunged away.

He laughed softly but didn't pursue her immediately. He was like a cat playing with a mouse. "I'll be gentle with you, Shell, if that's the way you want it. You know I can be."

She sought to enunciate her words clearly and to suffuse

every word with steel and concrete: "I will *not* get into some cheap physical affair with you, Heath Tanne . It would only make you despise me more, and frankly, I couldn't bear that. Not to mention the way I would feel about myself for giving in to you." She scrambled up from the rug in an attempt to escape the charged atmosphere.

Unhurriedly he followed her to the other side of the room and leaned arrogantly against the table. Again she felt the full impact of his physical presence, his negligent beauty. He was wearing a pair of tight jeans that clearly outlined every bulging muscle in his thighs. A simple, unadorned western shirt opened at his neck to reveal a mass of curling chest hair. His sleeves were rolled up to the elbows, and she stared in fascination as a dark-haired forearm reached out to take her hand gently.

She could fight his brutality, but she had no strength against this . . . this sweetness. Her heart began to beat against her rib cage like the wings of a frightened butterfly. He grazed his beard across her palm, then closed her hand over his mouth and bit softly. Her legs turned to water and nearly buckled. Only Heath could affect her like this.

"I want to make love to you on these cold lonely nights," he whispered thickly, his eyes turning dark and sleepy with desire.

She was drowning. A woman's sweet poignant need washed over her, wrenching the breath from her lungs and paralyzing her thought processes. In another moment he would take her in his arms and she would be lost. She groped for something—anything—that would save her. Her natural gift for sarcasm provided a suitable piece of floating wreckage to cling to.

"If you're so damn concerned about my lonely nights, then bring me a radio." It was all she could do to say this and make her body as stiff and unyielding as a poker. "I'm sure it would be just as entertaining."

"Damn you!" He jerked her forward and held her with one arm around her waist. "Why are you playing so hard to get?"

"Because I'm not cheap and easy as you so obviously think. Go let Christine satisfy your lust."

His black eyes glittered with anger. The hand around her waist tightened convulsively.

"I want no part of you as you are now, Heath. You're cold and calculating, and at this moment I think I hate you as much as you hate me."

He shook her as if she were a slender tree. "You owe me, Shelby."

"I don't owe you my soul!"

But he wasn't listening; he was forcing his body against her, pressing her breasts against his chest in a savage, hurtful embrace, and his lips were seeking hers in blind, angry frustration.

She fought him and managed to graze his cheek with her fingernails. This loosened his grip for a moment, and she hurled herself away and stumbled and fell before the fire.

"The answer is no!" she screamed. "Can't you get that through your thick, hairy head?"

"Why you . . ." He started forward.

Feeling faint, she closed her eyes, knowing that this time he would get his way. When after a moment nothing happened, she opened her eyes and found him putting on his coat. She experienced a strange confusion of emotions, not all of them related to relief.

After he finished buttoning the coat, he ran a distracted hand through his hair and started for the door.

"Heath!" she cried softly.

He halted but didn't turn around to face her. "Go to bed," he ordered in a strange brusque voice. "I didn't come here to rape you."

During the two weeks that followed Shelby spent hours alone. She did not see Heath at all. Joe Sam brought her weekly supplies of fresh provisions, and Dove came by once unexpectedly with a sack of newly picked Minnetonka apples from their backyard apple orchard. During this brief, almost silent encounter Shelby sensed curiously that Dove's opinion of her was not as violent as it had been at first, for even though she was by no means friendly, she was not openly hostile either.

Joe Sam never stayed more than a few minutes on his visits and spoke of his grandson only once when Shelby asked if Heath had gone back to Butte. Joe Sam explained that White Brave had gone on autumn roundup and wouldn't return for several days. She didn't know whether to be relieved or sorry.

At first the nightmares she suffered concerning her past relationship with him were excruciating, as if being brought near him had pitched her into a vast and terrible remembering that haunted and tortured her every minute. Then a strange process began to take place by degrees. In her enforced solitude and loneliness she was made to relive and examine what had happened so long ago—the poignant, never to be forgotten episode in the motel room and the terrible trial. It was as though reliving it by day freed her from the ordeal of having to dream about it. Her nightmares became less frequent, and slowly she gained a perspective on her own guilt.

During this time of the roundup, when Heath was miles away helping his hands cut out cattle for market, Montana was visited with a beautiful sixty-five-degree Indian summer. Shelby used this halcyon time to search the surrounding countryside for an escape route, always fearful of the wild, never venturing so far as to get lost.

Each sun-drenched day was clouded by failure and the depressing knowledge that Heath hated her and would continue to as long as he remained the stubborn and vengeful man that he had become. That he desired her sexually told her nothing. He was a passionate man. She had always known this. She had experienced it. She would not allow him to vent his passions on her and then throw her away as a broken and useless thing he was no longer interested in. She had been right to fight him off that night in the cabin and to subjugate that part of herself that needed him as the wildflower needs the warmth of the sun, as the flute needs breath to make it tremble with music.

She wrote to Luann, telling her all manner of lies, firm in her resolve not to involve her sister. A cry of help to Luann and Woody would bring an investigation by the police. Shelby was not prepared for that yet and doubted she ever would be. She simply could not damage Heath again, nor could she implicate Joe Sam, Aaron, and Dove in any wrongdoing.

She told Luann that she and Heath were getting along like two peas in a pod, blissfully happy in their rediscovery of one another. She wrote that she was his private secretary at his home office on his ranch, which sounded like a cozy arrangement, and explained why the postmark was from Choteau instead of Butte.

Joe Sam accepted the unsealed letter silently, refusing to read it. He merely tucked it into his shirt pocket and grunted, as if he knew beyond a doubt that she would not give the whole insane situation away in a letter to her sister.

She was astounded by the old Indian's astute ability to judge character. He was patently sure she was not going to do anything to get Heath in trouble. He was right, of course; nevertheless, she was still determined to escape. That dream was always before her as she longed for her family, her job, and the whole wonderful normality she'd known back in Florida.

Early one morning during the last few days of this beautiful mild spell, Shelby took a long walk, following the lush creek bank to the lake it fed. Montana had a wild grandeur that exhilarated yet overwhelmed her. She had been looking for days for the trail Heath's grandmother had taken on her trips between the cabin and the frame house. She took her favorite spot on the teapot-shaped rock overlooking the lake and luxuriated in the gentle breeze playing in her lustrous jet hair. No luck again today. Perhaps the trail was overgrown and now invisible.

Climbing down from the rock, she followed the creek upstream until she was deep in timberland. Douglas firs, lodgepole pines, and ponderosa pines spired into the sky like green coniferous cathedrals. The air was brisk but still warm for October, since Indian summer was still in residence.

She was determined to find that escape route today. She didn't know exactly how she was going to explain to the foreman and his wife her dire need to be taken to Choteau without incriminating Heath, but she would cross that bridge when she came to it.

Wearily she sat on some flat yellow rocks by the gently running creek and scoured the landscape with troubled azure eyes. This rugged and majestic country had a way of making one feel totally insignificant. Bending over, she caught some water in the cup of her hand and doused her throat, not caring that it wet her open shirt front and meandered on down in a half dozen trickling rivulets to soak her bra.

She got up and passed the damp hand across her forehead, deciding to climb the ridge and check around up there. Suddenly she stopped stock still, caught between uncertainty and blind panic. She had heard something—something inhuman—a low animal growl which set the hairs on her neck on end and congealed the blood in her veins.

She searched the surrounding rocks and caught sight of a huge cat blending cunningly into the tawny rock upon which it was crouching. She let out a dry, breathless scream and scrambled sideways into a hedge of thorns.

It might have been this sound of panic or the smell of fear that incensed the cat, for immediately he was springing through the air like a huge golden lightning bolt. Gunshot cracked closeby, nearly shattering her eardrums, and she screamed and twisted among the briars.

The animal hit the rocks immediately above her with a dull thud, then dropped off in slow motion, scattering gravel as he rolled down the slope to her feet. His eyes stared at her like huge dead agates and his hide twitched and rippled with the reaction of afterdeath. There was a neat scarlet hole in his head, and presently a sticky black sludge began to ooze from it.

Holding her stomach, she turned and doubled over. Afterward, she accepted a soaked kerchief from Heath's hand. She wiped her mouth, then, with the deliberation of one still in shock, carefully folded the kerchief and handed it back to him.

He put his arm around her shoulders, gently urged her out of the thicket, and made her sit by the stream. When her gaze again sidled toward the enormous dead animal, he spoke roughly, "Don't look."

Reaction set in and she began to sob uncontrollably. He dropped down and pulled her across his lap, hunching his muscled shoulders over her protectively until her crying subsided into a series of dry little whimpers.

Holding her head to his chest with one hand, he leaned over and again doused the kerchief, wringing it in a tight, trembling fist. "Here, let me see." He eased her head to his thighs and sponged the scratches on her face and arms.

"Damn, damn, damn!" he swore. Her eyes welled up and spilled over. "Don't cry," he ordered sternly. "I can't stand it when you cry." Bravely she blinked away the tears. He was reminded of that time seven years ago when he had ordered her to stop crying. Pain, and something he refused to identify, choked in his throat, and he swallowed and replaced them with anger.

"What the hell were you doing out here anyway," he exploded, "picking wildflowers like the other day when Dove tracked you down? When I think of what could have happened if I hadn't come along . . ." Words failed him, and fear drove him further into anger. "Haven't you been told time and time again to stay close to the cabin? Are you stupid or just hard of hearing?"

She rolled away and rose to her feet on unsteady legs. "I was trying to escape, if you want to know the truth," she informed him defiantly.

He levered himself to his feet, towering over her in a rage. "And you nearly did—right into oblivion. That wasn't your common garden-variety pussy cat, you know. That was a vicious killer. He could have mauled you to

111

pieces in a matter of minutes. Didn't I warn you there were wildcats out here?"

"Yes!" she spat, her own anger rising to match his. "You told me. And I thought you were kidding."

He jammed his fists into his waist. "You thought I was kidding," he repeated mockingly. "You're pretty damn dumb."

"Stop saying that. I'm not dumb."

"What else would you call it? You nearly got yourself killed!"

"Wrong!" She stabbed at his chest with her forefinger. "*You* nearly got me killed—because I wouldn't be out in this godforsaken wilderness looking for a way out if it weren't for you and your obsession for revenge."

"Oh no!" He shook his head and held up his palms. "You can't lay this one on me."

"You just won't take the blame for anything, will you, Heath? Not now or seven years ago. Everything is *my* fault, isn't it?"

"Yes," he hissed between clenched teeth. "Now let's get going. My horse is over there." He nodded to a stand of pine, and she saw his stallion's shiny black flanks.

She stole a glance at the felled wildcat, feeling a strange pity now that it was quite dead and harmless. "Why did it jump me?" she asked, skirting a wide circle around its gruesome head.

"It was doing what comes naturally," he explained curtly. "Looking for its dinner. Life out here can be very brutal."

She shivered uncontrollably and rubbed her arms. "Sometimes I love this country," she said, "and sometimes it frightens me."

"It's better than so-called civilization." He lifted her

112

without ceremony and threw her into the saddle. "At least everything out here is clear-cut. One either survives or he doesn't. The cities are full of dead men still walking around, not even realizing they are dead." He tightened the horse's cinch and went on, "Civilization has a way of stripping a man of his freedom—certain death any way you look at it."

"Oh, how can you be so cynical?" she cried. "You have everything a man could want—an education, a successful law practice, two airplanes to fly anywhere in the country, a huge ranch with a thousand head of cattle. You're incredibly good-looking, and I'm sure you could have any woman you fancied. What more could a man ask for?"

"Peace," he answered, swinging into the saddle behind her.

She felt sick again. "You could have that too," she argued quietly, "if only you would bury the past."

"I've tried." He pulled the reins and directed the horse toward the cabin. "It always resurrects itself like some evil ghost, to haunt and remind me that I hit a man and nearly killed him. All because of trying to defend a cheap little liar who wasn't worth the effort."

She exhaled raggedly and compressed her lips. His hand spanned her stomach, drawing her hips to fit more snugly between his legs. He touched her breasts and made her lean back. They rode together, his arm finally forming a circular bar of steel around her waist.

"Don't try to escape again," he ordered flatly. They had reached the cabin. His hands slid under her arms and lifted her down from the saddle. "You could never find the way to Choteau, and even if you could, it's too far. And if you've got it in your head to get my foreman, Dan

113

O'Neil, or one of the hands to take you out of here, forget it; I've told them you're my guest."

"They *know* about my presence here?" she asked in surprise.

"A couple of them saw you the other day when they were out looking for strays." He smiled without mirth. "They were smitten by you, Shelby. I had to tell them you were mine—all mine. So don't try to seek them out and get friendly with them. They think I've staked out a claim on you. Poaching on the boss's territory is unthinkable, much less driving the tearful little idiot to Choteau after a lovers' spat."

A cold wrath engulfed her. "Do you mean to tell me you've let all those men think I'm your personal . . . ?" She faltered at coming right out with the word.

"Yes." He nodded, laughing soundlessly. "I'm afraid so."

She struck out blindly and cuffed him on the leg, making absolutely no impact on the muscles of steel. The horse shifted but Heath controlled him easily.

"You don't give a damn about me, do you?" she cried.

"Did you give a damn about me?" he asked softly. "You didn't seem to mind when everyone thought I was a ravisher of young girls, a drunken brawler, and a jealous killer. I didn't notice you gushing with explanations to clear my name, to temper the jury's opinion of me. No, you merely looked at them with those big weepy blue eyes and convinced them I was a lustful animal who preyed on little girls."

"Then why didn't you make them think differently?" she shot back. "Why didn't you allow your defense attorney to tear me to shreds on the stand? You could have, you know. I was about ready to fly to pieces anyway. Why

114

didn't you get your revenge then, Heath? Why wait all these years for the coup de grace? Think of how good it would have made you feel to see me ripped up before the jury, exposed for what you knew me to be, a cheap little seventeen-year-old"—and this time she came out with it— "tramp! Oh yes, it would have been so satisfying for you. Your attorney could have made me tell how I used every trick in the book to tempt you into making love to me, how I even begged you to complete the act when you discovered I was a virgin and wanted to stop." Her arms were flying wildly as she was in a fine rage.

"Shut up," he growled lowly.

"No!" Her chin tilted up defiantly. "Not until you tell me why you wouldn't let your lawyer have a field day with me. I've always wondered about it. You must have known how shocked and repulsed the jury would have been to discover that the one time in your room hadn't been enough for me, that I sought you out begging for more, that . . ."

"Stop it." He slid quietly out of the saddle, but she ignored him.

". . . that I was offended when you weren't interested, and turned to the nearest bystander. They would have known then what a hero you are! A killer of grizzly bears and wildcats. A defender of foolish wantons about to be devoured by leering drunks. A noble prince!"

He grabbed her shoulders and shook her, grinding one phrase over and over between his teeth: "Shut up, shut up, shut up . . ." When he finally released her, she stumbled back and her arm came up to sweep thick swathes of hair out of wounded eyes and a face stark with hopelessness.

"A noble prince," she repeated in a despairing whisper, "who doesn't know the meaning of forgiveness."

He turned abruptly and swung into the saddle, sharply reining, and galloping across the prairie like a wrathful centaur.

She found a bottle of whiskey in the pantry, fixed a stiff shot, downed it in two gulps, then shuddered from head to toe. Her adrenaline gradually receded to the innermost regions of her body, leaving her with an empty depression. She found the first-aid kit and swabbed alcohol on her scratches, cursing this pain and every other pain.

Finding a way out of this morass of guilt and hate and revenge was hopeless; finding a way out of this thick Montana wilderness was hopeless. Heath's spiteful lies had obliterated any chance she might have in talking the foreman into taking her to Choteau. She was trapped. Trapped! In every way imaginable.

Wearily, she stripped down to bra and panties and went to bed, something she never did in the middle of the day unless she was sick.

A couple of hours later she woke up feeling as if she'd been caught under a fast-moving steamroller. She knew she should eat something, but being listless and deeply depressed, she didn't have the energy to do battle with the stove.

Upon hearing a soft knock on the door, she tied on her robe and shuffled lethargically to answer it, knowing it wasn't Heath, since timidly knocking on doors wasn't one of his virtues. Her unexpected visitor was Dove, looking shy and uncomfortable holding a plate wrapped in tin foil and a huge orange thermos.

"I brought you some supper."

Shelby's chin wobbled at this unexpected kindness. Dove acted as if she didn't notice as she entered the cabin and set the things on the table.

"White Brave said you nearly had an accident with a wildcat today. I thought you might be too upset to cook for yourself. I've noticed you've lost weight since you came; that's not good."

She took the foil from the plate to display a lovely arrangement of steamy home-cooked food. "Sit down. I'll fix you something to drink." She fetched a cup from the cupboard and filled it from the thermos. "It's soup." She smiled tentatively.

"You shouldn't have gone to all this trouble," Shelby protested tremulously.

Dove hid an expression of pity. Her heart had always gone out to helpless things. She was beginning to think of Shelby as a rabbit caught in a trap, yet at the same time she sensed keenly that Shelby had too much pride to want to be considered as such.

"I'll go now."

"Do you have to?" Shelby asked forlornly. Then she looked away, embarrassed by the note of pleading in her voice.

"No. I can sit and have a glass of tea with you if you'd like."

Shelby started to rise and get a glass.

"I'll get it." Dove halted her. "You go on and eat before the food gets cold."

"This looks very good. What is it?"

"Venison tenderloin."

Shelby took a mouthful and chewed thoughtfully. It was delicious. "Hmm." She took another bite. "I've never eaten venison. It's very tasty." Dove was a terrific cook; she had to give her credit. Besides the meat and gravy, the plate held saffroned rice, broccoli soufflé, and a huge buttery slice of homemade bread. Shelby's spirits began

117

to rally, and soon she was feeling something like herself again. Presently she realized that conversation between herself and Dove had practically become nonexistent.

"How did you get to be such a fabulous cook?" she asked inanely.

"Grandma taught me." Dove shrugged. "And I've had plenty of practice."

"How long have you been keeping house and cooking for Joe Sam and Heath?"

"Five years. Grandma died five years ago, just after White Brave was released from prison. It was as if she had hung on just long enough to see him again. I had already been out of high school for a year. Grandfather had wanted me to go on to college when I graduated, but I had had enough of boarding with strangers and studying subjects that held little interest for me. White Brave and Grandfather needed me; and I needed them We are a close family, even though White Brave and I have had our share of run-ins."

Shelby could well imagine that.

"My brother has always been wild and mettlesome, like an unbroken mustang. Grandfather is the only one who can truly handle him. And Grandma could too," she added, "when he was a youngster and she took her frying pan to his impudent backside."

Shelby stifled laughter, visualizing this most gratifying spectacle.

"But since White Brave came out of prison he has changed. He never laughs anymore, never tells jokes as he used to, or . . . or shares himself. He's become his own law, and sometimes Grandfather can't even reason with him."

"I've already asked Joe Sam, but I want to know from

you why he kidnapped me." Shelby said. She had finished her dinner and was tracing a square in the gingham table-cloth with her fork.

"He and White Brave had a terrible argument," Dove answered softly. "Grandfather had been after my brother for many months to get married and carry on the Tanner name. He's the only male left and Grandfather's only hope for immortality, so to speak."

"I see. And Heath doesn't like children," Shelby added resignedly.

"Oh, no! It's women he doesn't like. He has been very ruthless in the way he has treated them. As for children, White Brave loves them. He's taught all the children in the family to ride, and they think he's a combination of John Wayne, Superman, and a circus clown. His natural affinity for children is another reason Grandfather gets so distressed when White Brave speaks of never getting married. But Grandfather says White Brave says that because he still has feelings for you."

He has feelings, all right, Shelby thought. They can be summed up in two words: *monumental hatred.*

Dove sighed. "So, Grandfather, in his forthright Indian manner of dealing with things, suggested that he and Aaron bring you out here to see what it would prove. But I don't think he imagined White Brave would carry it as far as he has. He's been very upset with White Brave lately."

"Have they been quarreling over me?" Shelby didn't want the crime of pitting blood against blood added to her already long list of sins.

Dove shook her head. "Grandfather doesn't say much. He bides his time. But he's taken to smoking his pipe

119

again. He always smokes his pipe with a frenzy when he's building up to something."

Ironically, Shelby was distressed. The enigmatic old Indian might well be angry with her too. And for some inexplicable reason she couldn't bear that thought. "I hope Joe Sam doesn't feel too hard toward me for going out in the woods today. Heath told me there were wildcats, but . . ."

Dove held up her hand placatingly. "Grandfather knows you're green. If anything, he admires you."

Shelby couldn't believe it. Joe Sam couldn't admire the woman who had sent his grandson to prison. As Dove had said, they were a close family, and if anything was evident at all, it was Joe Sam's unwavering devotion to Heath. "Has he said he admires me?" she asked disbelievingly.

"Not in so many words," Dove answered, "but he has mentioned that you are made of the same stuff Grandma was—grit and vinegar and unholy fire. You won't take any of my brother's bull, just as Grandma wouldn't take anything from Grandfather."

"Heath told me that she had flaming hair and a temper to match." Shelby had already decided that she and Heath's grandmother would have gotten along famously.

Dove's eyes softened. "Yes, Grandma was really something. Every time I think of her I remember happy, crazy things."

Dove got up, reaching for the empty plate. "I have to be getting back. It's growing late and Grandfather will worry." Her braids swung over the table like ropes and got in her way. She flipped them behind her with irritation. "I hate my hair," she muttered, more to herself than to Shelby. "Braids are not stylish on a twenty-four-year-old woman, even if she is part Indian."

"Why don't you cut them off?" Shelby suggested impulsively.

Dove looked up, giving her the impact of a pair of solemn light brown eyes demanding total honesty. "Do you really think so?"

"Hey!" Shelby whispered softly. "I'm sorry. I had no right. I wasn't being critical. It's just that my sister and I were forever setting about fixing each other up. We were always turning her kitchen into a beauty parlor." My brother-in-law, Woody, never knew when he would come home to find that the smell of permanent-wave lotion had mingled unfragrantly with the aroma of stew. She laughed lamely to herself. "I guess I just got carried away."

Dove looked down at the tablecloth and continued to frown. "If I made these changes," she asked slowly and thoughtfully, "do you think Aaron would notice?"

Shelby's mouth dropped open in surprise, remembering the blond good-looking young man who had helped abduct her. "How do you know he hasn't already?"

Dove shook her head. "Not in the way I want him to."

Shelby smiled. "If you do with your looks what I think you can do," she averred, "Aaron will be bowled over."

Dove looked up seriously. "Will you help me?" she asked.

"You want me to do it!" Shelby exclaimed incredulously.

"Yes," Dove answered with the succinctness of one who has come to a definite and irrefragable decision. "I would not go to a strange shop to have this done, nor would I try to do it myself." She squinted at Shelby with honest appraisal. "While Grandfather has been admiring your spirit, I have been admiring your poise and style. I would

121

trust you if you would be willing to take on a hopeless case."

Shelby didn't take a moment to consider. "I'd love to. And you're not a hopeless case. You'll see." She was determined to prove Dove's faith in her was not misplaced. She was also determined to foster the friendship, however tenuous, that was growing between them.

Dove began packing the supper things into the bag. "White Brave is going into Choteau tomorrow for supplies. I'll go with him to shop." Her face was alight and her eyes had taken on a decided glow. "You sit down tonight and make up a list of the things we will need. I'll send White Brave by to get it before we leave in the morning."

"I wouldn't go into a lot of detail about this with Heath," Shelby warned.

Dove humphed. "The less he knows, the better," she agreed. "This is women's business."

After Dove left, Shelby rubbed her palms together gleefully. Having finished with the renovation of the cabin several days ago, she was eager for a new challenge. Transforming the willowy Dove into a thing of beauty would be both pleasant and gratifying.

As she sat down to make her list, however, and plan her modus operandi, she realized she was faced with certain seemingly insurmountable obstacles. How in the world did one go about giving a perm without running water? How did one style hair without a blow dryer? What would Heath's reaction be when his sister turned up looking like a brown-eyed, older version of Brooke Shields? There was no doubt in Shelby's mind that Dove had this potential.

Shelby decided she didn't care what Heath thought

122

about it. Dove had asked for her help, and her violent, despicable brother didn't enter into the picture. As for the lack of running water, they would have to make do with the rain barrel and water heated on the stove. Dove would have to draw upon the stoicism of her ancestors when the time came for her to put her head under the icy rainwater.

CHAPTER SEVEN

Gray dawn filtered through the dainty floral print curtains at the bedroom window as Shelby woke to an insistent tapping on the pane. Shelby got up on her knees and peered out, her hair swirling around her head like a smoky cloud, her gown gaping to display a long expanse of deeply cleft flesh.

"Open up," Heath ordered.

She scrambled off the bed and hurriedly opened the door. "Why didn't you just barge in," she asked, "like you usually do?"

"Don't start in on me this morning, Shelby." He strode across the floor without casting her so much as a glance.

She raked her hand through sleep-tumbled hair and her eyes glittered with blue ice. "What's the matter, did Joe Sam order you to be polite to me? What a pity. Now you can't come in here and maul me anytime you please."

"I'm not in the mood for one of our invigorating arguments, Shelby. Dove told me you had a list of items you needed. Just hand them over and I'll be on my way." His glance slid down her figure impersonally then back to her face. His appraisal was cool, as if she were a prize Hereford without brains or feelings.

She turned away, highly incensed. "Must you rush off

so soon," she said, acidly sweet. "It's so seldom I get a visitor out here, you know." She moved toward the stove and removed the plate to build a fire. The gown clung to her like thin gauze. "And what kind of hostess would I be if I didn't offer you a cup of coffee this early in the morning?"

"The list, Shelby," he repeated in darkening tones.

She tsked and laughed sarcastically. "Just like a man. Too busy to sit down and enjoy a companionable cup of coffee with an old friend." She knew she was baiting him. The part of her brain still operating on reason admonished her to hand over the list without further delay, but she stubbornly ignored it. "The coffee will be ready in a minute. It does take some time with this lovely little stove."

"Okay, Shelby," he whispered threateningly. "I'll accept a cup of your coffee and anything else you have to offer. But I'm warning you, honey, don't start something you can't finish."

She wanted to fling the list at him now and run and hide in her bedroom. But it was too late; she had started this little charade, and damned if she would back out. She became acutely aware of her lack of attire, and a rush of heat flashed across her back and prickled her hairline. She stood by the stove waiting for the water to boil and her color to subside.

He shrugged out of the coat and sat down at the table. Dressed in a pair of close-fitting jeans, expensive leather boots, and a western-cut shirt with white pearl snaps, he looked every inch the successful rancher, his well-groomed beard adding just the right touch of rugged machismo. Her heart lurched crazily as she turned with coffee cups in hand and was struck forcibly and unexpectedly by his blatant good looks.

She bent over the table. He tore his eyes away from her beautiful breasts and gazed about the room. In the blooming dawn light he became aware of the changes she had made in the cabin since he had last seen it.

She sat down, well away from him on the other side of the table, and stirred her coffee with a shaky spoon.

"Well, well, what have we here?" He waved his hand in sarcastic wonderment, nearly upsetting an arrangement of dried flowers at his elbow. "Oh, pardon me, Shelby." He grasped the arrangement between thumb and forefinger and very solicitously scooted it down the table to safety. "I nearly crushed your cute little basket of flowers."

Somehow this mockery hurt her more than anything had thus far. She had spent hours on this place. She had scrubbed and polished. She had broken fingernails. She had bent over the sewing machine until her back ached. No, it didn't look slick, like something out of *Better Homes and Gardens,* but she had tried—had given it her all. She took a sip of her coffee with white-knuckled hands, wanting nothing more in the world at this moment than to fling its contents into his bearded sardonic face.

Ignoring his own coffee, he stuck his thumbs in his jeans pockets and continued to ridicule her. "Yes sir, you've done a real fine job here. It's sweet. Real sweet. I expect the seven dwarfs to come hi-hoing in any minute."

She was on her feet instantly, nearly upsetting her remaining coffee. With convulsive movements she reached for a shelf over the the stove and grabbed a piece of stationery. "Here's the list!" She tossed it at him angrily "Now get out!"

It hit his chest, then fell to the floor like a wounded white bird. Slowly he unfolded his solid, massive body and stood up. "Just like a woman," he taunted, echoing her words moments before. "Inviting a man to sit down for a cup of coffee, then ordering him out when the kitchen gets too hot. What's the matter, can't you take a dose of your own medicine?" He advanced toward her slowly.

"There's the list, Heath." She pointed to the floor with a trembling forefinger. "Now pick it up and get out of here."

She backed away as he came inexorably closer. "You're shameless, Shelby," he taunted lowly. "Do you think I'm going to let you get by with teasing me like this without taking just a little taste of what you have been displaying so enticingly?"

She stifled a scream and turned and ran. Unfortunately, circumstances cornered her in her bedroom. Realizing her mistake, she turned to block the door, but it was too late.

"How convenient," he said, smiling without mirth as he glanced at the crumpled bed.

"If you don't get out of here, I'm going to scream bloody murder."

"Go ahead." He reached out and pulled her close to his chest. "Cry rape and make me feel guilty like you did before."

She struggled unsuccessfully. "How can you feel guilty when you don't have a conscience?"

"But I do." He grabbed her chin and forced her to look at him. "I've always felt guilty about what happened in that motel room seven years ago. I've always felt that I was responsible, that I should have known better. You used my guilt against me the other night when I came to you, didn't you?"

"I don't know what you're talking about."

He drew her closer, squeezing the breath from her body.

127

"Don't tease me, Shell. Don't play on my guilt and then tease me. Or I might do something crazy."

"You're already doing something crazy. This whole kidnapping scene is absolutely insane. When they locked you up, they should have thrown away the key."

With a muffled exclamation, he threw her on the bed and pinned her flailing arms and legs with his weight. "You just never know when to shut up, do you? You insist on driving me beyond control even when I have the best of intentions."

"You haven't had any good intentions for years."

"Really? Then maybe I should start right now."

His mouth covered hers and she steeled herself for its brutality. But his kiss wasn't biting and hurtful; it was gently controlled, every soft movement designed to thrill her sensually. When she opened her mouth involuntarily, his tongue entwined with hers until red hot flames burned behind her eyelids and she felt she was losing her soul.

"You're mine now." His kisses were bathing the hollows of her face and neck. "My prisoner. And I'll do what I want with you."

"No!" She fought his shoulders with her fists. "You just want to hurt me."

"Does this hurt?" He slid the gown away and filled his massive hand with a swelling breast. His head bent and he suckled the tender, sensitive tip lusciously.

Desire, painfully intense, radiated from under her throbbing breast and shot through her like hot molten lava. Her fists became caresses, in his hair and down his wide, solid back. When he pulled down the remains of her bodice, she turned with a whimper and offered him her other breast, which he lifted to his face and took with fiery teasing kisses.

128

His hand lifted her gown and found that she was melt-ing with need. He caressed the softness of her thighs with sweet gentle strokes and then increased the pressure of his hand against her more deeply. A moan tore from her soul and shattered the air with its urgency.

"Oh, Heath," she cried softly.

He stroked the length of her legs while he nuzzled her breasts with his soft lips, driving her to the peak of release, but refusing to take her beyond. Wildly he kissed the side of her face and her neck, his teeth sinking briefly and with gentle savagery into the soft creamy flesh. Her fingers clawed at his shirt and pulled at his wide rawhide belt with weak, helpless insistence.

"Do you want me, Shell?" he whispered against her neck as his hand traveled again to her secret warmth.

"Oh yes, I want you."

There was a cessation of movement during which she lay quiet and bewildered. And then he laughed. His soundless, hot laugh seared her neck and covered her with humiliation. He pulled up and looked at her through two narrow black slits. "Don't ever cry rape to me again, Shelby, because you've just proven how willing you really are." His dark hair clung to his sweat-sheened brow, and he edged off the bed with weak, slow movements. "Why, if anyone was in danger of being raped just now, it was I."

Shocked, she pulled the sheet over her trembling body and stared at him with tragic, wounded eyes. Speech was impossible, but her expression told the depths of her deg-radation and shame.

As he looked down at her, his face contorted briefly with pain and self-loathing. Impulsively, his arm reached out. "Shelby, I . . ."

"Don't you touch me!" She recoiled, on the brink of

hysteria. "If you set out to prove I'm a tramp, you've done it. Now go away."

He gritted his teeth and swallowed thickly. Then he turned and left. It wasn't until after she heard the dying roar of the jeep that she gave into bitter, racking sobs that made her feel black inside and soulless.

"I hate you," she cried defiantly. "I hate you!" But she knew it was a lie. She loved him and had for the past seven years, or perhaps since the beginning of time. Her fear of what he could do to her took on monumental dimensions. He could make her his slave, then destroy her with cruel rejections like the one just a moment ago. He could put her in an emotional dungeon from which she could never escape, never see daylight. Already she was sinking, bending to his will. And there was no love in him to make the surrender sweet and beautiful as it should be between a man and a woman. There would be no cherishing, no deep, strong bond. He would laugh as he had done just now and trample her heart in the mud of rejection and despair.

"I have to get away," she whispered into the tear-soaked pillow. "Oh God, I have to get away somehow."

The next morning Dove arrived, and Shelby helped her carry in two bags of cosmetics and grooming paraphernalia. When asked if Heath knew what was going on, the tall, lissome young woman informed Shelby that her brother had left earlier in the plane for Butte and had no knowledge of what they had planned.

Thinking of Christine, Shelby asked if he was going to Butte on business or pleasure and was painfully relieved to hear that Heath's trip was precipitated by a call from Aaron regarding an important case coming up in court.

He needed Heath's advice, and plans had been laid for Aaron to accompany Heath home for a quiet weekend of work to clarify the case further.

Dove sat sacrificially immobile as Shelby loosed her braids, brushed out her fine, waist-length hair, and decided what was to be done.

"Are you very sure?" she asked, biting her lip. "It must have taken years to grow this."

"I'm positive." Dove set her face in grim determination. "Grandma insisted on the long braids. But I'm sure if she were alive today she'd agree that it was time to get rid of them."

Shelby sighed and took up a pair of sharp, gleaming scissors as a brave surgeon preparing for the first incision. "Just sit still," she murmured. "This won't hurt a bit."

The scissors snipped and snapped, and foot-long strands of brown silk began gliding down Dove's back. "I'm giving you a shoulder-length cut," she explained, clipping her words in time with the scissors. "Then I'll layer it all the way to the crown."

Totally absorbed in the creative process, she talked on in a monotone, ignoring everything except the task of transforming the raw material on Dove's head into a work of art. She crouched and bent and brandished her scissors.

Dove's glance fell to the floorboards, which were now covered with a shiny rug of interwoven chestnut-colored ribbons. She wavered slightly but forced her eyes to look straight ahead, away from the carnage Shelby was trampling underfoot.

"Now for a sweep of bangs," Shelby said in a business-like, self-confident tone. "You're going to look like a lioness when I get through."

Dove relaxed and let Shelby's confidence infuse her.

Within an hour Dove's hair was done all over with rollers and end papers. She had taken it all stoically except for the perm lotion, complaining with a curse that the smell was enough to curl your ears as well as your hair.

The rinsings were a labor of love on Shelby's part. Not wanting to expose Dove continually to the frigid contents of the rain barrel and the brisk Montana air, she had brought rainwater inside in a tub and had warmed it with water from the teakettle. Dove bent over the sink while she patiently poured pitcher after pitcher over Dove's bound curlers.

When the curlers were undone, Shelby exclaimed delightedly. Dove's head was covered with long wet corkscrews. She hastened to assure a skeptical and slightly panicky Dove that this was the way it was supposed to look wet.

She made Dove sit in front of the fire and began to pull the brush through her hair with long curving strokes. "You'll be able to do this with a hair dryer much easier," she said. "But for now, the heat from the fire will have to suffice. Conditions aren't exactly ideal here."

"Aren't your arms tired?" Dove asked softly.

"No. I'm fine. You do have a blow dryer at home, don't you?"

"White Brave does. He won't mind if I borrow it." Dove closed her eyes like a kitten being stroked and let the fire warm her cheeks and eyelids. "At least I don't think he'll mind. He's been very touchy lately. Grandfather is dreadfully concerned for him."

Shelby humphed inwardly. And well he should be, she thought. His grandson was a madman, determined to push Shelby in the same direction. Closing her mind to her inescapable predicament, she deliberately changed the

132

subject. "Don't you find it very lonely living out here in the middle of nowhere?"

"Sometimes." She shrugged then and added thoughtfully, "Yes, frequently, especially after one of Aaron's visits. But I've never been a social butterfly. White Brave says you are."

Shelby continued to brush Dove's hair silently.

"Well, are you?" Dove asked.

"Not the way he thinks," she answered sadly.

Dove stared into the fire, catching Shelby's melancholy mood. "If it weren't for Aaron's visits I would feel totally isolated. He breathes life into me."

Dove's hair was now magnificent, a tumble of wanton waves. It was the same length as Shelby's but without the sleek smoothness.

"My God, where did it all come from?" Dove asked as she gazed into the mirror.

"You like?" Shelby asked with a smile.

"I'm speechless."

"Just remember to brush it out and away when you style it." She rubbed her palms together. "Now where are those cosmetics? I can't wait to start on your face."

"You make it sound as if I need plastic surgery."

"Hardly. Your features are strong, but they're perfect. You want to look good for Aaron tonight, don't you?"

They exchanged sly women's smiles as Shelby took up the tweezers and advanced on Dove's eyebrows. She plucked them, then smeared Dove's face with cleansing lotion. This was followed by a creamy, butternut foundation and earth-tone shadows and highlights. She explained each step in detail down to the application of the mascara and ended the job with a patient outlining of Dove's full lips.

Dove stared directly into Shelby's eyes as she applied the cinnamon-red lip gloss. "Grandfather was right about you. He told White Brave that you were as lively and sweet as the Montana sky in the summertime. He said in the very old days a brave would have given all his winter pelts and his finest horse to obtain a squaw like you."

Shelby found herself pleased and flushed slightly at this unusual compliment. "And what did Heath say to that?"

"White Brave called Grandfather senile, then slammed out of the room like an angry bear."

Shelby nodded as if she expected this and looked up at the ancient beamed ceiling.

"Grandfather has said on several occasions that you are a very strong woman."

Shelby put her hands on her hips and wagged her head disconsolately. "I hope to hell he's right."

"I have also come to believe that my brother's opinion of you is wrong." Dove squinted eyes, now dark and expressive and perfectly made up. "I feel that there is more to what happened seven years ago than White Brave knows, and I think he's a fool for not hearing you out."

"You're very perceptive." Shelby felt overcome with pain and she blinked at the age-old timbers above her head. "I made a lot of mistakes seven years ago. I was young and foolish and much of what happened was my fault. I have paid for those mistakes over and over in my own private way. But Heath doesn't understand about my actions at the trial. He doesn't know the pressure I was under. I tried to tell him about it that first day in his office. And I tried to apologize. But he wouldn't listen." She looked down and her tears spilled over. "Please believe me when I say I'm sorry for what I did to Heath. I didn't mean it."

134

She wiped her face and realized with horror that Dove's own eyes were glistening, dangerously on the verge of tipping their contents onto her perfect face.

"Don't you dare cry," she ordered sternly. "Don't you dare destroy all my hard work."

Obedient, Dove fluttered her lids rapidly and the moisture evaporated.

She wouldn't allow Dove to help with the cleanup. Aaron would be arriving soon, and Dove would need the time to bathe and change into one of the pretty new outfits she'd bought.

The equipment and magical potions were stowed in the jeep, and although Dove was too reserved to hug Shelby ecstatically as Luann would have done, her expressive look of gratitude and love had the same effect.

CHAPTER EIGHT

The door opened and vibrated alarmingly as Heath nearly slammed it off its hinges. Ready for bed, Shelby was sitting before the fire listening to some faint sad music on the radio. She dropped her head to her bent knees with a weariness beyond anything she had ever experienced, then lifted it again with a tired silent curse that she had been too busily engrossed in her chores to remember to lock the door. Not that it would have mattered. Heath was like a black tornado. Locked doors were nothing against his diabolical force.

"What the hell have you done to my sister?"

She pulled the reins of her inner resources, which like beasts of burden had scattered and faltered. "It's late and I'm tired. Why can't we discuss Dove tomorrow?"

"We'll discuss her right now!" He flung off a short belted leather coat, and Shelby's brows contracted painfully at the sight of him. It was the first time she had seen him dressed in the role of the smart, successful attorney. Her blue, miserable eyes devoured him hungrily as a deeper part of her remained encased in resentment and fear. He wore a gray three-piece, vested suit. His shirt was white and still crisp, and a beautiful, extravagantly colored tie was pinned against its front with a gold clip. Matching gold and ruby cuff links gleamed at his wrists. This sartorial excellence was only further accentuated by the rugged handsomeness of his dark head and the stubborn strength of his bearded jaw.

"Then by all means pull up a pillow and we'll discuss her. Sorry I can't offer you a royal throne." She reached for a velvet pillow and set it beside her, taking time to plump and pat it.

He flipped it away with a gleaming leather toe. "The hell with that! Just tell me where you got the utter audacity to paint my sister up like some trollop right off the streets."

"Trollop?" Shelby lifted her delicate creamy face innocently. "My, my, what an outdated, Victorian term. Your mind does work in a single groove, doesn't it? A single, *warped* groove. I don't suppose you ever refer to the lovely Christine as a—what was the word?—trollop. And I am assuming she uses all the modern artifices women do in order to attract a man. As a matter of fact, I'm sure she uses that and a lot more in order to captivate a man of base instincts such as yourself."

Cursing beneath his breath, he squatted next to her, thrusting his face nose to nose with hers. She caught the scent of his aftershave and the elusive, wild smell of his body. She breathed deeply and inhaled his clean warm breath. Her senses reeled and a sleepy liquid desire churned in the lowest part of her abdomen.

"Let's leave Christine out of this."

"Yes, let's do. I was merely saying that Dove has the right to make the most of herself."

"And you call diking up like some streetwalker making the most of herself?" he asked with angry incredulity.

Her anger rose to match his. "Oh, come off it! She looks

137

good and you know it. She left here today looking like a New York model."

"All I know is that she's not the same Dove. She served us dinner tonight in a clingy, revealing dress, totally uncharacteristic of her, she keeps sending Aaron promises with her eyes, and she walks differently—much differently. She has knocked Aaron completely off his feet. I couldn't get a bit of work out of him after supper. He kept going back into the kitchen to check on her like some moonstruck schoolboy." Having grown tired of squatting, he eased to a sitting position and unfolded his long, muscled legs slowly, as if they were aching. "I don't like it. I don't like it one bit. I've suspected an undercurrent between them for some time. I wish it had remained deeply buried."

"Oh, you're too much!" Shelby hissed angrily. "You're really too much. What right do you have to wish your sister a life of martyrdom to you and your grandfather?"

"As much right as you have to encourage her to dress up and act like an I-don't-know-what," he retorted savagely.

"She's twenty-four. She's not your little kid sister anymore; she's a grown woman who knows her own needs and desires."

"Damn you for interfering with my family like this!" His black eyes shone with anger. "Dove is too inexperienced to be falling for a man like Aaron. I know how he operates. I've seen him do it plenty of times. Dove is completely out of her element."

"So you and Aaron have gone out tomcatting together. So what?" she shot back furiously. "That doesn't mean he's as cold-bloodedly calculating as you are. That doesn't mean he can't have warm, genuine feelings, really care, really fall in love." In a white-hot fury, she started to get up, needing to be away from him, if only just across the room.

He grabbed her. "And what do you know about it, little Miss All-American? If they gave medals for what you provide, you'd be covered with them. What do you know about genuine feelings?"

She kicked and struck out blindly. He pinned her arms to her sides and leaned into her to subdue her struggles. He searched her face—the pristine, flawless features, the thick raven hair that could cover a man's chest like warm midnight.

"Are you going to prove what a beast you are and finish the job you started yesterday?" she asked.

Her trembling lips were provocative. He stared at them, then grazed them with his thumb to test their soft mobility. "I want to," he whispered. "God, how I want to. I want to make love to you over and over until you scream for mercy. I want to move you so deeply that you admit no man has ever touched you as I have."

He turned his head sideways and fitted his mouth to hers, lightly, perfectly. She nearly swooned as his tongue made a stealthy, unexpected invasion and stroked the inside of her cheek. When he lifted his head, his lips were wet with her helpless, drugged surrender. His hand closed over her breast, and he bent to softly bite her lower lip.

She clenched her lids and gave a quiet sob. His hand left her breast and came to cradle the back of her head as if she were a baby. "Why do you do this to me? Why do you drive me to anger and then tear me apart?"

She buried her face in his warm shirt and silky tie, weeping silently.

"Don't! I can't stand it." He pushed her away roughly

and got up to prowl the room like a restless animal. "Do you know what Grandfather says about you? He says you're just like Grandma. That you're the type of woman who can bring a man to his knees."

Shelby sat up, wiping her cheeks with her palms. Heath circled the room again and ran his hand through his hair. "I told him he was a sentimental old fool. You're not like Grandma at all. Except for your sharp, acid tongue and audacity."

"I gather she kept you in line pretty well," Shelby remarked caustically. "For that alone I regard her as a heroic figure of majestic proportions."

Swearing softly, he stopped pacing, flung his suit coat back, and placed his hands on his hips. "I'm going to tell you something, you damn little smart aleck. And you'd better listen and listen closely. Only a thin thread of something I can't define keeps me from carrying you in there . . ." he thumbed toward the bedroom, ". . . and taking what I want with devastating thoroughness."

She blinked at him stupidly, fear sealing her lips.

"You remember that the next time you want to make one of your sarcastic comments." He grabbed his jacket and flung it over his shoulder. "And if I hear of you encouraging Dove with any more of this silly, romantic nonsense concerning Aaron, I won't let you off with a simple but frank male to female pounding. I will throttle you, Shelby. With my bare hands."

He wrenched the door open and slammed it brutally behind him. She continued to stare at it long after it had ceased shuddering. He had rendered her mute, but he had not subdued her defiance. She picked up a pillow and hurled it at the door with all the force of her hostility. "Bastard!" she exclaimed. The pillow hit the door with a muffled poof and dropped soundlessly to the floor, some-how symbolic of her effectiveness against him.

The gods were merciful, or perhaps her own body had grown weary of the constant upsets and nervous crises. Whatever the cause, she passed an unusual, dreamless, night. She had not been sleeping well and she had not been eating well. As further evidence that her body was rebell-ing against all it had been subjected to, it woke her the next morning demanding to be fed a hot, well-balanced break-fast.

She had just put the last of the dishes away when Joe Sam arrived in the jeep with the news that her sister had called and wished to speak with her. The enormous break-fast began to revolve sluggishly in her stomach. She felt an overpowering sense of dread. Something was wrong. Luann wouldn't have called unless it was important.

"Don't panic, Summer Sky," Joe Sam said calmly. "There doesn't seem to be an emergency. Your sister sounded anxious but not frantic. I assured her you would return her call within the hour."

The trip to the big house was brief. Shelby was too distraught to note how brief and how this might bear on possible escape later on. Joe Sam ushered her to the phone in the living room, explaining that Aaron and Heath were closeted in Heath's office working on a case, making the telephone in that room unavailable.

Dove came out of the kitchen and gave Shelby a wor-ried, silent smile. Shelby noted that she still looked like a model, wearing close-fitting designer jeans and a feminine white blouse. She allowed Dove a brief grin before her face clouded with anxiety.

Shelby dialed her sister's number and stood beside the

141

phone tapping her foot nervously while waiting for an answer.

"Hello! Luann?" she practically shouted into the receiver.

"Oh, Shell. It's so good to hear your voice. I was just getting ready to call you again. How is the romance of the century coming along?"

"The wh—? Oh, fine. Great!"

"Well, if Heath is as nice as his grandfather, you've certainly gotten yourself a catch. Mr. Tanner was so concerned when I called earlier. Such a mild, sweet man."

If Shelby hadn't been so steeped in worry, she would have laughed. Joe Sam mild and sweet? Well, in a way perhaps. "Look, Lu. I know you wouldn't have called all the way across the United States if something weren't wrong. Are you ill?"

"Not exactly," her sister confessed in a tired, wobbly voice. "I'm pregnant."

"Pregnant! But that's wonderful. I'll bet Woody is overjoyed."

"Woody is happy, of course. But Shell, you know how sick I get right at first. I feel about as low as a pancake. And the kids are right at that stage where they are constantly into everything. I-I just wanted to talk to you be-because it's all got me down."

"Oh, Lu, you had me to help before, didn't you?" Shelby remembered when Luann had been pregnant with Jeffie and Joanie; she had been so pale and listless and downright nauseated all the time.

Luann tried to be bright. "It'll pass. In a couple of weeks I'll be adjusted, and from then on I'll feel fantastic. That was the way it was with the twins. Smooth sailing after the first bout of sickness."

Shelby moaned. She felt like crying for her sister, who was so far away from the help she so much wanted to give her.

"Now don't you get upset. I didn't call to get someone boo-hooing with me."

"Does Woody do anything to help you?" she asked.

"Oh yes. He bathes the kids at night and cleans up the kitchen. Oh, please don't think I called to talk you into coming home," she rushed on. "You must stay out there and make those marriage plans with Heath."

Shelby rolled her eyes toward the ceiling. Her sister, the incurable romantic, had taken a few very necessary white lies and had expanded them into a forthcoming wedding.

"I just felt I needed to talk to you, to hear your voice. You know . . . I miss you. We were always together in tough times."

Shelby could hear Jeffie and Joanie in the background, howling about something. "Lu, you're going to have to put your foot down with those kids. They are going to have to be a little more considerate now that you're not feeling well."

"I don't have the energy to put my little toe down, much less my foot. If only I could get some rest," her sister whimpered into the phone, barely audible now as the battle, or whatever Jeffie and Joanie were engaging in, became more vociferous. "A week or two to pull myself together." Suddenly there was a horrible crash. "Oh no! Look, sis, I've got to go. They've just shattered a glass all over the kitchen floor. Don't worry about me. Really, Shell. 'Bye."

Shelby hung up slowly, biting her lower lip in agitation.

"I couldn't help hearing," Joe Sam said quietly. "I gather your sister is feeling ill and that her two youngsters, being the very active type, are not helping matters."

Shelby squared her shoulders. "Joe Sam," she said in a steady voice, "I must go to my sister if she doesn't get better very soon. She's the only one in the world who truly loves me. I can't stay here when she needs my help. You, of all people, should understand that, feeling the way you do about family ties."

It didn't seem as if he had heard her. He was sitting at a parquet table, his shoulders hunched over a gigantic jigsaw puzzle. He picked up a piece, tested it, and put it down quietly. Then he did the same thing with another piece.

Shelby cast a helpless look in Dove's direction. Dove wrung her hands in her tea towel and supported Shelby with compassionate, understanding eyes.

"Joe Sam!" Shelby addressed him again more strongly. "I can't let my sister down. She brought me through some pretty hard times and now she needs me to do the same for her. You are the only one who can pull rank over Heath in this ridiculous kidnapping scheme. I can't believe you won't do it now that my sister is sick and wants me with her even though she won't come right out and admit it. I can't believe you would be so cruel and heartless."

His eyes remained hooded. Saying nothing, he picked up another piece of the puzzle. It was as if she were trying to reason with a stone or an ancient redwood statue.

"Grandfather!" Dove cried passionately.

Joe Sam held up a gnarled hand to silence her. He raised his head reluctantly. "Go back into the kitchen, Dove. And trust me to handle this with Summer Sky in my own way."

144

Dove sighed and Shelby heard her muffled footfalls. The old Indian thoughtfully picked up another piece of the puzzle, his brow furrowed in deep concentration.

"Oh, Joe Sam," Shelby cried in a low, desperate voice. "Can't you see how futile all this is? Heath will never come out from under his cloud of hatred. He's enjoying it too much. He's . . ."

Joe Sam held up a leathery forefinger to squelch her in the same authoritative way he had Dove. His other hand slid the piece of puzzle smoothly and neatly into place. It was only after accomplishing this that he raised his head to focus her with a steely look of determination. "Wait a few days. If things aren't better with your sister, I'll fly you back."

Her knees buckled and she slumped down in a chair. Relief flooded over her in a brisk, all-consuming wave, leaving in its wake an inexplicable sadness. She would soon be free. Free! She would soon be in Florida—hundreds of miles away from Heath. Her heart stopped and her mouth turned dusty.

"Thank you. Thank you very much," she managed tremulously. She realized he was watching her closely, his eyes black, clever, shrewd.

"H-he'll be better off when I'm gone." She expelled a painful breath and sagged a little. "I-I remind him of too much. I-I make him behave badly," she choked miserably. "He's changed into something awful."

Joe Sam had gone back to his puzzle. "Down deep he is the same individual I named White Brave so long ago. He is still fine and good—and brave."

"Maybe you wouldn't think so if you told him how you were going over his head and taking me home. Then you might see his fine, brave temper!"

She thought he chuckled but couldn't be sure. "You must take pity on me, Summer Sky, and keep our little arrangement a secret."

A bud of suspicion popped open in her brain. He fitted another piece of the puzzle into place before getting up to take her back to the cabin. Dove stopped them with a questioning glance as they came through the kitchen, and Shelby reassured her with a smile and a nod. Joe Sam merely mumbled something about how good the roast smelled, then carried himself along unhurriedly on his amazing, slightly bowed legs.

Once in the jeep, he took some leisure time to pack his pipe and fire it up with swift, sure draws. He seemed lost in thought. But it wasn't anxious thought, for he was totally relaxed, almost smug. Shelby was extremely nonplussed now. The old Indian totally baffled her. He hadn't asked her to remain quiet about their deal because he was afraid of Heath; there was another reason, one she was at a loss to figure out.

After crossing the distance between the house and the cabin, he brought the jeep to a halt and Shelby climbed out. "What have you got up your sleeve, you crafty old devil?" she blurted impulsively.

He blew a cloud of smoke, and she couldn't see his face, not that she could understand anything in its stony, fixed features anyway. "Ah, Summer Sky, you're distrustful. This cuts me deeply."

"You just remember your promise to take me home."

"I always remember my promises, Summer Sky. I will take you home if your sister doesn't start feeling better very soon." With pipe set firmly between his teeth, he shifted to reverse, then leaned forward to speak to her again. "By the way, I like what you did to Dove."

Her mouth dropped open in astonishment as billows of smoke again enveloped his ancient, formidable head. She stepped away as the jeep swung backward then zoomed away at a purposeful steady speed.

The next morning, while her icy bedroom was still shrouded in dark predawn shadows, the buzzing of the telephone disturbed her sleep.

"Hello," she mumbled into the receiver, befuddled and half-frozen. "Who is it?"

"It's Heath," came his curt angry reply. "Who did you think it was? The President of the United States?"

"Oh, Heath, do y-you h-have to st-start in on m-me so early?

"I just wanted to inform you that your little plan worked—Aaron and Dove eloped this morning."

"Y-you're kidding!"

"And I can't even go after them since Grandfather left last night for parts unknown. I own two planes and don't even have the use of one when I need it."

She put an icy hand to her forehead. "Where did Joe Sam go? When will he be back?" Had the inscrutable old Indian run out on their deal? He wouldn't have done that, she assured herself distractedly.

"I haven't the foggiest. All I know is that I'm stranded here without the means to go get Dove and bring her back."

She dipped under the covers with the receiver in an effort to find warmth. "Why don't you just stay out of it? They're not two dopey teenagers, you know. Th-they know their own minds."

"Grandfather is going to blow his stack when he gets

back and discovers Aaron has made off with Dove like this."

"If Joe Sam is as om-omniscient as everybody says he is, he would have se-seen this coming weeks ago," she argued through chattering teeth.

"Are you cold?" he asked suddenly, changing the subject.

"I'm freezing, if you want to know the truth of it. It must be nearly zero in here. I hesitate to jog your memory, but if you'll recall, this godforsaken hole isn't blessed with proper heating."

He fell silent for a moment, then ordered brusquely, "Pack your clothes; you're coming here to live."

"That's insane!"

"You're from the South, Shelby. Grandfather and I already discussed the advisability of moving you in here during the hard winter months. Your stubborn pride will offer you very little comfort when it really gets cold." He paused. "And it does get well below zero here in the winter. I won't have you dying of pneumonia before . . ."

"Before what? Before you get your revenge?"

"I was going to say, before your sentence is up."

"Same thing. I can't and won't live in the same house with you."

"Are you frightened of me, Shell?" he asked with silky satisfaction. "Can't you take it?"

"No, I'm not frightened, you inconsiderate swine!" she lied explosively. "But I won't have you trying to maul me every minute of the day."

"What about every minute of the night?"

"That's cute. Real cute."

"Pack up, Shelby," he ordered in an exasperated tone of finality. "I'll be there in twenty minutes."

He spent the morning moving her and her belongings into the crimson room. He said very little during the whole process, but his every movement emitted black, unholy anger. She knew that he was upset predominantly with Dove and Aaron and Joe Sam only secondarily, for leaving the ranch without discussing his reasons. And then, underlying everything, were his feelings for her, which were nothing less than volcanic in intensity.

"I have to go over to my foreman's house to discuss the winter feeding of the cattle," he informed her, entering the crimson room unannounced.

"'Bye." She raised her hand and wiggled her fingers. "Are you going to lock me up before you leave?"

He prowled to the dressing table, lifted her compact, then set it down quietly. "No. You'll have the run of the house."

"Big of you." She squinted her eyes and smiled.

"If your nimble little mind is planning escape, forget it. I've disconnected the phones, and I'm using the jeep. Rosey, the gentle mare, hates cold weather and will not take you three feet from the barn. My black stallion is a one-man horse; he would undoubtedly throw you a mile and break your lovely little neck."

"You seem to have thought of everything," she remarked, unperturbed. She had already decided not to take any action. Joe Sam would come back in his own good time and fly her out. She had developed an unshakable faith in him; all her instincts assured her that he was a man of his word.

Heath became wary. She sensed his puzzlement and it amused her. Restless and thoughtful, he circled the bed and came around to the other side, where she was sitting. She glanced up; his jet eyes were alive and watchful.

She gave him a broad, jeering grin. "Don't worry, darling. I'm not going to try to escape today. You have my word on it."

"Your damned word isn't worth a plugged nickel. You're the most wantonly convincing liar I've ever met in my life. You don't know the meaning of honesty and you never have."

"You haven't let me be honest!" She shot away from him and went to the window.

"Oh spare me, please. I gave you a chance seven years ago, and everything that came out of that gorgeous mouth was a deceitful lie. You lied about your age, you lied about your experience, and you lied about me when you got on the stand."

"I did not!" she argued hotly. "I did not perjure myself on that stand."

"No. You didn't perjure yourself," he agreed in a quiet rage. "You merely damned me to nearly two years of hell by not volunteering the truth. That makes you a liar, Shelby, the worst kind."

She hugged her arms and trembled. "And what are you, Heath? Have you ever analyzed yourself? I think if you did, you would find a hateful, vicious man—a man who won't listen to reason, a man who won't love or allow those around him to love. Right now you are livid because your sister has found love and has reached out to embrace it. You're mad at Aaron because he has given himself to love, even at the risk of displeasing you, his friend and partner."

"Bull!" he exploded. "That's a lot of sentimental hogwash! Love is a meaningless four-letter word—a trite label people stick on various kinds of emotions." He walked toward her, his large body tense and menacing. "Yes, I'm

150

angry with Dove and Aaron. They've behaved stupidly, and I want to bite nails every time I think about it."

"You're the stupid one." She poked a trembling forefinger at his chest. "You're a blind, stupid bast . . ."

He gripped her arms and shook fiercely before she could finish the word. "Don't you curse me! Don't . . . you . . . dare . . . curse me," he growled, punctuating each syllable with a head-shattering jar.

When she thought her head must surely become unhinged from her neck, he picked her up bodily and hurled her toward the bed, where she landed and bounced several times in a confusion of arms, legs, and black flying hair. As the bed stopped moving she looked up and wiped the hair out of her face. He stood over her breathing heavily, his hands two tight, vengeful fists. Silence hung in the air thickly.

Gripped by cold fury, she opened her strawberry-tinted lips and lowly and with perfect distinctness intoned the hateful word he had ordered her not to say.

His hands shot out, grabbed her again. She lunged away from his attack and managed to scramble off the bed. By now she was sobbing earnestly, and a part of her was crying for him more than herself. He caught her around the waist and hauled her back onto the bed.

"Go ahead and turn on the tears. They won't work this time because this time I don't care. I don't care."

She stopped struggling and lay pliantly in the circle of his arm. They could have been lovers. They would have been lovers if it weren't for everything else.

"Don't hurt me." Unconsciously she touched a trembling hand to her uncovered arm.

He saw the defensive movement, the soft vulnerable quivering of her breasts, and the ugly bruise weltering on

151

the white fragile skin. "Oh God!" he groaned, clenching his eyes against the visible results of his wrath. He rolled to the edge of the bed in an agony of self-loathing. "Did I do that?"

"You're incredibly strong, Heath. You could break me in two."

"If you know that, then why do you goad me, drive me beyond control? I need to be rid of you," he admitted softly and without anger.

"If I were in Florida, you would be rid of me."

He pressed his thumbs to the corners of his eyes. "No. Distance has nothing to do with it." He turned and allowed his satin black eyes to rove over her at will. He held her limp hand and leaned forward.

She experienced an uncontrollable fear, then a burst of sensation as his bearded cheek grazed caressingly against her lips. Then his mouth softly kissed the bruise on her arm, and then withdrew. He left the room silently, his anger spent.

CHAPTER NINE

Late that evening she heard the drone of an airplane engine and deduced that Joe Sam was arriving home. She set about making a pot of coffee and pulling things out of cupboards in preparation for supper. Now that Dove was gone, she assumed she would be taking over the role of chief cook and bottle washer.

The front door opened and she heard children's excited voices. Amazed, she dropped what she was doing and ran to investigate. It was Jeffie and Joanie, muffled to the ears in winter clothing. Behind them stood Joe Sam, wearing his usual immobile expression.

"They've come for a visit," he explained simply as Shelby's sky-blue eyes went wide with astonishment. "I'm going to my room for a rest now. It has been a long journey for an old man."

The children clamored for her attention, both talking at once. As she knelt to hug them and unzip them from their padded cocoons, Joe Sam wearily walked to his room, his shoulders drooping from fatigue.

They were hungry, so she gave them cookies and milk. She drank a cup of coffee and listened to their chatter in fascination. She was able to piece together that Joe Sam had visited Luann and Woody early that morning and had somehow convinced them to allow the children to come out for a two-week vacation in Montana with their Aunt Shelby. The wonder of it was that they had trusted the mysterious old Indian enough to go along with the idea.

Reaction had settled in her mind in layers. Uppermost was the fresh, sunshine joy of being reunited with the children. Underneath that, she seethed with frustration and resentment. In bringing the children out here, Joe Sam had eliminated the need to take her home. And very deeply buried, in a small chamber secret even to herself, lay a tight little ball of relief, for as attractive as escape from Heath was, the ultimate parting would have been like separating her heart from a piece of itself.

She unloaded the children's luggage from the jeep and put it in the room next to hers. Upon unpacking she found a note from Luann explaining that she had included every shred of warm clothing the children possessed and fussing that they had nearly outgrown their last year's hooded parkas. At the bottom of one of the suitcases was a huge box of cereal which, Luann had explained, was their latest culinary passion. Apparently they would eat it three times a day if one would let them.

Shelby bathed them, dressed them in their warmest pajamas, and gave them a good, well-balanced supper of hot food, even though they tentatively suggested having Frootie Tooties. They were obsessed with the promise of snow and kept asking Shelby when the sky was going to open up and let it fall. She assured them it would happen any day. With dreams of sled rides and snowmen, they bedded down and drifted into a snug, warm sleep.

She went back downstairs, fixed a tray of hot food and a carafe of coffee, and took it to Joe Sam's room. He was sitting fully clothed in front of his window at a low, round table smoking his pipe thoughtfully. She saw that the bed was mussed and knew he had just gotten up from a nap.

"I've brought you some supper." She set the tray on the table in front of him.

"Thank you." He put down the pipe and turned to the food. "That was very considerate of you. Where is my grandson?"

"He's been at the foreman's house most of the day. He insisted that I move in here this morning since the weather turned so cold last night." She sat down on the edge of the bed and gave him an intensely baffled look. "You're an excellent kidnapper, Joe Sam. First me, and now the children. They told me the whole thing. You are quite an operator."

The corners of his mouth lifted slightly before he took a mouthful of food. "You're sorry I brought them out here?" he asked, chewing words and food at the same time. "You're not glad to see them?"

"I'm overjoyed and you know it. Having the kids is like having a patch of spring in the dead of winter. But this was a very clever move to keep me here, Joe Sam. I just hope you know what you're doing."

He lifted the carafe and poured out some coffee. "I only know that I couldn't let you go back."

An exasperated snort conveyed her own feelings on the matter. "How did you find my sister?" She changed the subject abruptly.

"Pale. She had that washed-out look women get the first few months of pregnancy. The two weeks of rest will do her good." He fired up his pipe again and leaned back in the chair. "Despite her condition, however, she was quite talkative."

"Oh yes, Luann goes a mile a minute." Shelby smiled. "Sometimes Woody gets very aggravated with her."

Joe Sam's black eyes glittered through clouds of smoke. "She was extremely happy that you and my grandson were getting along so well. She asked how much longer it would be before the wedding."

"Oh," Embarrassed, Shelby looked up at the ceiling. "I'm afraid I let her believe that."

Joe Sam puffed quietly.

"Well," she said defensively, "I had to tell her something. I could hardly admit you all had kidnapped me."

"True," he agreed. "I shudder to think what your brother-in-law would have done with that piece of news." His glittering eyes bored through her to her very soul. "Which just goes to prove my first impression of you was correct, Summer Sky. You are a strong woman. And very protective." The glitter took on a spark of amusement. "But the question is, who did you want to protect? Your family? Or my grandson?"

"Since you're so smart, you figure it out."

"I have."

She got up to retrieve the tray from the table. His smug composure aggravated her. "Dove eloped with Aaron this morning," she quipped lightly in a malicious attempt to completely shatter him. Let him put that in his pipe and smoke it!

"Good," he grunted between contented puffs. "I gave them my consent yesterday. They certainly didn't waste any time, did they?"

"Don't you ever get excited?" She opened the door to to leave. "Just one time I'd like to see you really break loose and show some emotion."

156

"I'll tell you what, Summer Sky. I'll wear a great big smile on your wedding day."

"Ha!" She exited, slamming the door irritably.

The next morning Heath came into the kitchen as Shelby was fixing the children their favorite breakfast. He was dressed in boots and jeans. Over his checked western shirt he wore a bulky cardigan sweater that made him even larger and wider than he was. His shiny black hair and dark auburn beard made him seem rugged and bear-like.

Joanie took one look and retreated behind Shelby, holding on to her hips for dear life. Jeffie, bigger and braver, focused first on Heath's boots, then gazed up his tall frame as a midget taking in the extent of a giant. He finally met Heath's black eyes, which were dancing with amusement.

Head thrown back, the intrepid boy asked in a bold voice, "Are you a cowboy or an Indian?"

"Both." Heath smiled down at him.

"Both," Jeffie breathed in a small, awed voice. "Wow!"

"This is my nephew, Jeffie, and my niece, Joanie," Shelby said, trying to prize Joanie loose.

"Grandfather told me about them late last night," he said, moving across the kitchen to pour himself a cup of coffee.

"Children, this is . . . er . . ." How should she introduce Heath? They called Joe Sam Mr. Tanner, so that was out. "This is White Brave."

"White Brave," Jeffie echoed breathlessly, even more impressed—if that were possible.

"That's my Indian name." Heath laughed. "But you can call me Uncle Heath. It's much friendlier. Welcome to the Bar-T." He shook Jeffie's small hand, then peered

157

around Shelby's pelvic region to catch a glimpse of Joanie, a very beautiful little girl with black curly hair who looked up at him with one fearful blue eye, the other being pressed into her aunt's backside.

"I thought I saw a little girl around here a moment ago," he mused, nonchalantly taking a sip of his coffee as he perused the room. "I was going to ask her to go horseback riding after breakfast, but I guess she has disappeared." He went over and sat at the table. Jeffie immediately joined him. Joanie sidled out from behind Shelby and slipped silently into a chair. He smiled at her, and she gave him a beautiful, blue-eyed expression of shy approval. His heart turned over as he saw a fragile, miniature Shelby sitting before him.

"You can have some of our favorite cereal for breakfast," Jeffie offered magnanimously. Joanie smiled her agreement.

"Oh, I don't think Heath . . . er . . . Uncle Heath would find Frootie Tooties as tasty as you all do," Shelby interjected. "He would probably prefer bacon and eggs."

Heath, however, was not about to jeopardize his tenuous relationship with the children by rejecting their generous offer. "I'd love some cereal this morning."

Shelby set the table, and they all prepared to feast upon Frootie Tooties. "You asked for it," she murmured as she poured his bowl full of blue, purple, and pink smiley-faced bits of cereal dotted heavily with star-shaped marshmallows.

As they ate the strange fruity concoction, the children chattered gaily about everything from snow to spurs, and the milk over the amazing colorful mixture turned to a nauseating shade of lavender.

"Isn't this yummy?" Joanie asked, beaming at Heath.

Realizing that his answer might be crucial to their future rapport, he gulped, "Terrific."

Joanie smiled at him fully then, with adoring blue acceptance.

In the days that followed, the children dogged Heath like little puppies, chafing unhappily when he shut them out of his office while he worked and opening up like little wildflowers when he came out to play with them. A lovely made-to-order snow fell. He took them on sled rides and taught them to build snow forts. He told them Indian stories after supper, then switched to cowboy tales before bedtime.

Shelby watched this tender, charming Heath with amazement, and something swelled up inside her and threatened to explode and drown her with its intensity. This was the real Heath—the kind, sensitive man she had fallen in love with seven years ago.

At odd times she would catch him staring at her as she dressed the children or mopped them up or scolded them after playing too long in the snow. His expressions were unreadable, as if held behind a mask.

One afternoon she put on her red coat and went outside to watch them in one of their rough and tumble games. Jeffie ran up, pelting Heath fiercely with snowballs. He grabbed Jeffie and deftly rolled him in the snow as Joanie attacked from behind, gleefully anticipating her turn.

"Help us, Aunt Shelby!" Jeffie cried. "You're not going to let him get the best of us, are you?"

"Certainly not!"

A huge snowball fight ensued, with a great deal of running and throwing of snow. It turned into a battle royal between Shelby and Heath after the children ran off to play in their snow fort. Finally, Heath grabbed her arm, threw her into a drift, and rolled her as easily as if she were Joanie; then he turned away laughing in triumph.

She got up quickly. "Not so fast, you big gorilla!" She jumped on him full force as he turned around in surprise. They both toppled into the snow laughing, she pinning him down with her body.

Suddenly they lay very still, panting in unison and staring at one another. He turned over on top of her, burying his cold nose in the side of her face, breathing deeply.

"No, Heath, please. Not in front of the children."

He raised his head and closed his eyes, hovering over her briefly before getting up to walk toward the house.

The night before the children were scheduled to leave, Joanie woke up crying from a nightmare. Shelby went to her, gathered her into her favorite blanket, and helped her downstairs so that her frightened fussing would not wake Jeffie.

She took the child into the darkened living room and drew her on her lap, trying to soothe and comfort her, for she knew from experience how frightened and alone one feels after coming out of a bad dream.

"I want my daddy," Joanie cried, snuffling convulsively. "I want my daddy."

Heath appeared from his bedroom, which adjoined his office and also the living room, wearing only a pair of jeans. Strange attire for the middle of the night, thought Shelby. Then she realized with an odd sensation that Heath must be one of those men who slept in the raw.

"What's wrong?" he asked, running his fingers through his dark hair. "Is she ill?"

"No, just a bad dream. Go back to bed. I'm sorry we disturbed you. It's probably a good thing they're leaving tomorrow. She has missed Woody dreadfully—they're very close."

"Fathers and daughters usually are, aren't they?" he commented.

"Not always," she answered briefly, thinking of her own father.

Joanie's crying had quieted to intermittent, watery sniffles. "Would you take care of her while I fix her something warm to drink?" Shelby asked.

"Sure." He wrapped his arms around the tousle-headed, fragile-faced six-year-old replica of Shelby and sat in his grandfather's rocker. She gave him a blue, wide-eyed, grateful look, dropped her head on his chest, and closed her eyes.

By the time Shelby got back with the cocoa, she was fast asleep and Heath was looking down at her tenderly. "Look," he whispered.

Shelby peeped at Joanie's little urchin face, framed cutely with dark curls and a battered blanket, then took the cocoa back to the kitchen.

Heath eased out of the rocker and went upstairs with her, Shelby following close behind his broad naked back. He carried her down the dark upstairs hall into the darker bedroom where the children slept. She didn't stir when he tucked her gently into bed.

"It just takes a man's touch," he whispered, leading Shelby down the hall to her room.

She opened her door and light from the crimson room flooded around her, outlining her body through the filmy material of her nightgown.

She turned smiling, oblivious of the filtering effect the warm light was having on her modest apparel. "Thank

161

you for being so good to the children." Impulsively, she reached to caress his bearded face.

His eyes filled with a slow, black-velvet agony. His hand trembled in the charged atmosphere and came to rest tenderly against the side of her breast.

"Oh Shell, I want you so much."

Her hand curled around the back of his neck and pulled gently. He stumbled forward, pushing the door closed and locking it with stunned fingers while his head swooped down at the same time to devour her hungrily. He kissed her everywhere flesh was exposed, blindly, out of control, his body a powerful fountainhead of unrequited passion.

His ardor staggered her, and she was powerless to deny him, her own breathless need taking over her total being with a mindless, towering insistence of its own. Her hands became lost in the silkiness of his hair, the muscled warmth of his shoulders. And she cried his name softly, whimpering, when he freed her lips long enough for her to do so.

He fumbled with the buttons of her gown then swept it down her creamy shoulders, standing back to watch as it drifted airily to the floor. "I've wanted to see you like this," he whispered through a constricted throat. "A thousand times I would have given my life to see you like this."

Calmer now, and as if in a trance, he reached out to worship her with his hands. She touched him in return, her palms flat against his chest, trembling outward and down to brush his heaving ribcage and his tense stomach muscles. For a few moments they were like two blind people, matching touch for touch. When she was frustrated by the material of his jeans, her eyes locked with his in silent helpless pleading. Slowly he obliged her and it was

162

as she had suspected: he had been wearing nothing under the jeans.

Now their bodies fused together in a searing embrace, and there was nothing to hold them back. No clothing, no thought for tomorrow or yesterday. They were lost in one raging, all-consuming fire with the same need, the same goal. He lifted her and placed her on the bed and their passion doubled as they fought to kiss one another where their hands had touched, driven to roughness, their open mouths wide and burning.

Their ultimate consummation was natural and unplanned, uncontrolled yet beautifully orchestrated. It was as if they had become one person, with one beating heart —one body with the same pulses, pleasures, and soul-soaring satisfaction.

When Heath eased a little away to make her more comfortable she buried her face in his shoulder.

"Don't cry," he ordered softly.

"I'm not." She wasn't anywhere near tears; she was filled with wonder and love for him, and she felt that the present moment was the only reality in the universe.

Still holding her close with one arm, he leaned toward the bedside lamp and clicked it off. Then he nuzzled his head to her breasts and sighed contentedly.

"I thought you were leaving." She cradled him close and he wrapped his arm around her hips possessively.

"Not until I have to. Not until daylight drives me out." Inhaling languidly, he grazed his bearded cheek across her nipple, then took its succulence in his mouth.

Heath was gone and it was late morning when Jeffie and Joanie came into her room to pull her up by the arms. Shelby had to get up to fix their breakfast and pack their suitcases, for today they were leaving for home. She rose sluggishly, slightly achy, as her and Heath's lovemaking had taken its toll on a body not accustomed to such activity.

Their stolen night of ecstasy had been beautiful and awesome. Shelby hugged its memories to her with a smile. But the smile didn't last long. In the cold light of day, what she had allowed, consented to freely, in fact, broke in on her with the force of a tidal wave.

She was his prisoner now in the truest sense—in the only way a man can truly make a woman a prisoner. Last night he had enslaved her to himself. Just the thought of him made her heart thunder with love and her arms ache to hold him.

She knew now why great kingdoms had warred and powerful and talented individuals had thrown themselves in the dust for love. Love could be the most beautiful or the most destructive force in the world. Heath could destroy her now. As his unwilling captive, she could fight him, but after last night she belonged to him completely. She had to leave. It was her only hope of saving what little of her heart she could salvage.

After breakfast she quickly and efficiently packed the children's things. Then she went to the crimson room and inexorably, with slow, deliberate movements began to pack her own clothes. When Jeffie came in to ask her what she was doing, she informed him that her visit was over too and that she was going back with them.

She didn't stop to think what Heath's reaction would be, she didn't want to. Perhaps last night had satisfied his male proclivities to conquer and possess. Perhaps in the cool, passionless aftermath his desires had turned to disinterest and derision. Her heart writhed in her breast and clenched like a fist at the thought.

She clasped her suitcase shut and set it on the floor. Dove and Aaron would be arriving anytime now. They had agreed to take the children home to Orlando as Aaron wanted his father and mother to meet his new bride. Heath had apparently agreed to this belated honeymoon, and Shelby suspected that Joe Sam had in his own quiet way managed to bring his grandson around to a measure of acceptance concerning the marriage between his partner and his sister.

Suddenly the door of her room burst open and slammed shut. She was confronted by Heath, who appeared to be in a towering but tightly controlled rage. This was the first time she had seen him since the unutterable wonder of what had taken place between them the night before, and she nearly swooned as visions of their intimacies burst in her memory like warm liquid lights.

"Jeffie tells me you're packing to go home," he rumbled lowly.

"Jeffie told you right. I'm going."

"Like hell you are," he contradicted softly. "I don't know what gave you the idea I would agree to this little maneuver, unless it was your very convincing performance last night."

"You got what you wanted," she choked painfully. "I'm not going to stick around here and let you into my bed every time the urge strikes you. I don't like being used!"

He flinched as if she had struck him. "You used!" He stabbed at her with a wrathful finger. "That's very funny. You were hardly the vestal virgin offering herself up as a silent and inert sacrifice. If I remember correctly, you actually pulled me into this room." The muscles in his arms bulged tensely and his breathing became ragged. "So

165

don't play the martyr. You made love to me like a little wildcat. I have the scratches on my back to prove it." He advanced toward her in a black, angry prowl. "You left marks, Shelby! Do you want me to strip and show you where?"

She stooped against this callous onslaught and covered her fiery red cheeks with her hands. "Stop it! I hate you for this."

His head jerked slightly and he came to a halt. "Hate me then, Shelby. But realize without the slightest doubt that I will not let you go. Don't come down those stairs with your suitcase, or you will cause me to make a scene Jeffie and Joanie will most definitely not understand."

Shelby descended the stairs empty-handed. She had explained to the children that she had changed her mind about going home with them, adding wryly that Uncle Heath needed her here.

Dove ran into the warm house with Aaron close on her heels. She hugged Joe Sam first and then Shelby. Shelby saw with a deep and unaccountably poignant pleasure that marriage had turned Dove into an even more lovely woman than she had been before.

Joe Sam warned them that he suspected a big snow was coming. He wanted them in the air very soon, for his keen senses had told him it would be a terrific storm.

Aaron admitted he had heard on the radio that a blizzard was headed their way. "I just have to give Heath this trial report." He pointed to a manila envelope in his hand. "And then we'll be off."

"Are these the children?" Dove exclaimed, looking down as Shelby zipped them into their winter cocoons.

"Yes, Jeffie and Joanie. My two favorite kids," Shelby answered.

"They're adorable! Joanie looks just like you."

"My sister and I look a great deal alike, and Joanie has taken after us."

Heath came out of his office and walked into the front room. Aaron extended his hand and Heath took it reservedly. "You certainly pulled a fast one."

Dove went into her brother's arms and gave him a big hug. "Don't be angry," she pleaded. "We knew you would put up an argument if we told you our plans. Grandfather knew. And we thought you needed time to get used to the idea."

"You'd just better take good care of her," Heath threatened his partner in a low voice.

"I know how to treat a woman," Aaron countered in steady tones.

Their eyes locked, and Heath's face became granite. Joe Sam broke in on what appeared to be mushrooming into something of a confrontation. "No time to lose. You must get into the air quickly," he urged, "or you won't be able to fly out at all today. Then it might be several days before Dove gets a chance to meet her new in-laws."

The children raced out to the jeep and climbed in. Dove settled them in comfortably and positioned herself as close to the driver's seat as possible, waiting for Aaron. He deposited the luggage in the jeep and then slowly walked back toward Heath, who was standing on the front porch with Joe Sam and Shelby.

Shelby waved good-bye to the children and blew kisses with her gloved hand. Joe Sam stood aside in a plaid mackinaw. Heath had foolishly come out without a coat on and stood hunched against the bitter wind as he clutched the trial report under his arm.

"So, Tanner-Tate can add another acquittal to their collection," he remarked to Aaron.

"Yes," his partner answered in a gruff voice. "But what I have to say to you, Heath, has nothing to do with that trial." He pointed to the envelope. "It has to do with another one—the trial that took place seven years ago in which you were the defendant."

Joe Sam broke in. "Aaron, this isn't the time. In a matter of minutes the storm will break over us in vicious blankets of white."

"I have enough time to say what needs to be said. This has been on my mind and it haunts Dove constantly. I want it off my chest before I face my father and Shelby's sister."

"What are you talking about?" Heath growled.

"I'm talking about my part in this . . . this travesty of justice." His regretful look pierced Shelby. "I'm sorry," he said in honest apology. "I wish you would forgive my part in this . . . this *ridiculous* escapade. Dove wants you to forgive the way she treated you at first. Can you?"

Shelby shrank back against the storm door and nodded wordlessly.

"I was wrong about you," he went on. He turned to his partner. "And I was wrong about you."

Heath flinched visibly.

"You were guilty seven years ago. Shelby's testimony had nothing to do with that. The jury's verdict was correct. You committed a crime. Face it and stop blaming Shelby for something you yourself did. *You* are responsible for your actions, not her. Every man has to accept the consequences of what he has done. Perhaps they are

168

harsh—sometimes too harsh. But blaming it all on some-one else is not the answer."

Aaron caught Shelby's pained expression, then turned back to Heath. "Let it go, Heath. Don't let the past destroy you as a human being."

Heath turned his back on his friend and went into the house, his entire bearing indicating a high degree of rage.

Aaron gave Shelby a long and steady look. "What a pity. I think you're really in love with him. I wish to God I'd never brought you out here." He turned and walked to the jeep.

Shelby caught Dove's somber eyes, smiled softly, and waved. Dove lifted her fingers in a silent salute of love and sadness. At that moment they became sisters, and Shelby felt as close to Dove as she did to Luann.

Heath hibernated in his office for the rest of the day, while a swirling white blizzard raged outside. Shelby was despondent. The house was now devoid of the gaiety of the children. Its silence and Joe Sam's silence filled her with a strange sense of doom.

Dove called to inform them that they had made it safely to Butte but would have to wait until morning before departing for Florida since heavy snow had cut visibility to near zero. She got off the line quickly, as she wanted to call Luann and let her know about the delay.

By midafternoon Shelby had turned on the lights in the house and had started supper. Joe Sam was still in the living room, thoughtfully working on his huge jigsaw puzzle. The silent calm in the house was unnerving.

She felt shaky inside, as if waiting for something terrible to happen. She made a fresh pot of coffee and took some to Joe Sam. Then she carried a cup into Heath's office. He was sitting, in the dark, at his desk with his head in his hands. Papers were spread all around in confusion, as if he'd intended to work but couldn't.

"I brought you some coffee," she whispered as if in a tomb. "Supper will be ready soon." She reached out to touch his shoulder.

He drew back violently at this contact. "Get away from me," he warned in a very deeply troubled voice.

"H-Heath," she said brokenly, "I-I'm so sorry about what I did to you. God! Can't you forgive me!"

"You're sorry!" he snarled. "How sweet that you're sorry! You send a poor slob to prison and you're just very damned sorry. A woman is sorry when her cake turns out lopsided or her hair doesn't look right. What the hell is sorry?"

"Heath, please listen . . ."

"Shut up!" He bolted to his feet and flung the coffee cup and saucer off the desk; they smashed into a dozen pieces.

She cowered momentarily, then drew herself up to meet him face to face, using every ounce of courage within her to do so, for if she was ever in danger of being struck by him it was now.

"All right," she challenged. "What do you want me to do? What can I do to make it up to you? Slit my wrists? They say that blood atones for sin. Is that what you want? Blood? My life, perhaps? Why don't we get Joe Sam to build us a cross and have a regular crucifixion? Would that make you happy?"

"Get out! Just get the hell out of here and leave me alone."

She raised her her proud, beautiful head. "Fine. I'll leave you alone. I'll leave you to the cold comfort of your hate." She walked to the broad oak door and turned. "Good-bye, Heath," she said in broken tones of despair.

Joe Sam tried to catch her as she crossed the living room, but she eluded him.

"Summer Sky."

"It's futile, Joe Sam. Face it and take me home after this storm. You must, in the name of common decency."

He started toward her but she ran up the stairs, suppressing silent hysterical sobs.

CHAPTER TEN

Heath had told her to get out and that's just exactly what she would do. She would leave his beautiful house and never step inside it again. She would go back to the cabin, and if Joe Sam was half the man she thought he was, he would take her home in the very near future. Even the quiet, monolithic faith of the old Indian must be shaken by now. Even he must have accepted at last the man his grandson had become.

She zipped up her red parka and tied the hood securely, the white fur framing a face streaming with tears. She pulled on her gloves and then her boots, having to sit on the bed to do so and crying afresh at the memories of her and Heath making love there not many hours before.

Going through the living room, she heard sounds of arguing from Heath's office. Poor Joe Sam. Wouldn't he ever give up? Upon opening the door, she was met by an arctic blast that froze the tears on her face and turned her sobs to icy vapor.

She had never known such extreme cold. It assaulted her violently and made her bow and fight and claw her way to the barn. She had already decided to ride Heath's black stallion to the cabin. He was fast, and she didn't want to be out in this bitterness any longer than necessary.

The horse seemed gentle enough as she saddled him. Heath's warning that he was a one-man horse had probably been a lot of hogwash designed to frighten her.

The barn was frigidly cold and smelled of manure and fresh hay. Shelby worked quickly before she lost her nerve and reversed her decision. Walking back into the house like a whipped puppy unable to brave the cold was unthinkable at this point. Heath would be only too happy to ridicule her or subject her to his intense anger again.

She eased the horse through the barn door and noticed with dismay that the storm had intensified. The horse shied at the stinging gray blizzard and tried to bolt away. She spent a few moments grappling with the door, the rearing horse, and her own trembling fear, finally managing to bring all three under control.

By the lights from the house and the position of the barn, she got a fix on her direction, mounted the horse, and headed toward a destination impossible to see. The horse stepped gingerly, and his neck and head fought the reins. She let him have slack and urged him along gently with her boots.

By now she couldn't see three feet ahead of her and was really frightened. Realizing speed was of the essence, she spurred the horse sharply. He darted forward and then stopped stiff-legged, bucking her into the air.

She landed, unhurt, in a huge drift, the cold shock of the snow hitting her face and seeping under her collar, stunning her momentarily. She pulled herself up, staggered, and began to brush herself off.

The horse was nowhere in sight, not that she could have seen him even if he had been close-by. Dread wrapped its icy fingers around her heart. She knew and accepted without question that the horse was gone. He had undoubtedly gone back to the barn. She would have to make the rest of the trip on foot.

Lifting a gloved hand to her eyes, she tried to get her bearings. A swirl of snow whipped around her head and tore off her hood, raising the hair off her neck and freezing her backbone. She grabbed it with shivering hands and tied it back on. Her teeth began to chatter, startling her with their foolish noise. She was cold. Colder than she had ever been in her life. She couldn't see the way to the cabin; she couldn't see the mountains in the distance or the tamarack nestled at their feet. She couldn't see the huge black shadow of the barn or the warm glow of the lights in Heath's house.

She was lost. And the world was a confusion of blinding snow. She began to run and call for help. Her legs had become as blocks of ice, clumsy and unwieldy and disobedient to her commands. Her blood was congealing in the frozen veins of her outer extremities and in self-defense had begun to slowly and painfully withdraw itself to the warmth of her heart and her vital organs.

Fear of death smote her from within and made her wild and panicky. Her legs tangled and she fell, sobbing and crying the only name she had ever cried. "Heath. Oh, Heath! Please come and find me."

But the man she loved and hated so intensely didn't magically appear. She lay quietly in her tunnel of snow. What would he think when the blizzard died and he came to unearth her? Would he experience grief? Sorrow? Would he shed just one tear on her behalf? Would he wish he'd treated her differently?

She began to feel almost comfortable. She supposed she was too numb now to be troubled by the cold. Breathing lightly, she closed her eyes sleepily and imagined herself back in Florida. It was summer and the sun was hot. She smiled. She was on Clearwater Beach, lying on a blanket in the hot, blazing sun. Sleeping, drifting into oblivion.

Someone kept calling her name like a buzzing, bothersome fly. She lifted her gloved hand to brush it away. She would be a marble statue tomorrow, a shiny marble statue, translucent like ice. But now she was fine. It was just like the beach. So warm and cozy. No need to breathe. No need to think.

"Shelby! Oh my God. My God!"

Heath had come after all. He was jostling her with his panic. She didn't want to move, so she didn't. She refused to please him by moving.

He begged her to be alive and he prayed. There was something desperate in his prayers that made her want to cry. So she cried. Silent, blistering tears that scalded her stiff face and made her come to full consciousness.

"Oh, Heath." She reached for him instinctively and clung to his neck.

He lifted her and somehow got them both mounted on the horse, laying her across his chest and protecting her face from the raging storm. He held her as if he would never again let her go.

Carrying her into the house, he put her gently on the utility room floor while Joe Sam closed the door against the blizzard. They both knelt down beside her. Joe Sam forced her to take a large dose of whiskey, after which he made her take more. Heath pulled off her boots, which were full of snow, while Joe Sam examined her face and hands for frostbite.

"How is she?"

"She'll have some pain," Joe Sam answered grimly.

"But she's alive. Give her as much whiskey as she'll drink. I'm going to see to the horse."

Heath tilted the flask and poured the vile, smelly stuff down her throat until she gasped and shoved his hand away.

"If you give me any more of that, I'll throw up," she choked weakly.

"That's my Shel." He gave a shaky laugh. "That's my beautiful fighting woman."

"The horse threw me," she mumbled numbly. "I couldn't see a thing . . . didn't know where I was." She closed her eyes and slipped away again.

Quickly he stripped off his layers of clothing until reaching his jeans and undershirt, still dry and warm. He removed her parka and saw in anguish that her clothing was clinging to her skin soaking wet from the melted snow. Shelby hadn't known the necessity of layering clothing before going out in weather like this. He grabbed the whiskey again and force her to drink a little more.

He lifted her and took her to her room, agony and shame and compassionate love working in his face. He lay her limp form on the red carpet, ran the bathtub full of warm water, and turned on the electric blanket. Then he came back and knelt down. Drawing a deep breath, he peeled off her wet jeans and then her shirt. Pausing only briefly, he gently and with trembling hands, divested her of her underthings. She became coherent and began to hit out at him with futile, impotent arms.

"Don't fight me, Shell. Please." This was more a whispered prayer than an order. "You need help; you need me."

"Stop! You can't see me like this." Her very slender arms moved over her naked body defensively, trying to

176

hide areas too exposed, too lush to be concealed. "Oh, Heath!" she cried miserably.

"For God's sake, Shelby!" he pleaded. "I'm trying to save your life."

"No. I can take care of myself." Her words were sluggish from the cold and slurred from the effects of the whiskey. "Leave me alone. Go away."

He lifted her tenderly, effortlessly. "Trust me. I'm begging you, Shel. I have to put you in warm water. You might die of hypothermia if we don't get your blood circulating and your body temperature back up."

She whimpered and hid her face in his chest. "My feet, my hands—they're hurting. A million needles."

"I know." Then he repeated in a softer voice, "I know. I went through this once when I was a young boy. The pain is dreadful, but only for a while." He lowered her gently into the water. She lay back, all modesty drowned in pain, and began to cry.

"Don't," he groaned.

"Why not? What else is there?"

"The pain will subside soon. Think of that." A shaking hand cupped some water and smoothed it over her shoulders and breasts.

She closed her eyes and sobbed openly. "My pain will never go away."

He washed her eyes with gentle clumsiness, and new tears replaced those he had rinsed away, bathing her face with a warmth of their own. Beneath his gently stroking hands the blood in her feet and legs began to thaw and she writhed in discomfort.

"Just a little while longer, darling," he crooned. "Soon you will feel better."

"No I won't," she contradicted. Her head lolled to one

177

side. "I'll never feel better," she repeated in a meager whisper. "This is awful."

"Better to be here," he said, "than out there making a beautiful statue of ice."

"*You're* the statue of ice," she accused, her eyes flying open and blazing blue fire. "Deep inside you lies a heart of impenetrable white ice. You're the eighth wonder of the world—a glacier man."

He was amazed. In her present extremely vulnerable state, she could still defy him. He lifted her from the water and held her close while reaching for a towel.

"I hate you!" she said fiercely, then broke off with a sob. "I hate you, Heath Tanner," she choked vehemently.

He swayed momentarily like a stunned animal, catching his lip between his teeth and clenching his eyes briefly. "Go ahead and hate me then. At least you're alive."

"Yes," she agreed. "Quite miserable, but alive."

He wrapped her in the towel with warm intimate hands, then lifted her in the cradle of his arms. "Where's your nightgown?" he asked, standing her next to the bed.

"In the bureau drawer over there." She pointed with a shaking forefinger.

He was back in a moment with a long flannel garment, the only concession to practicality he'd made when buying her lingerie. It was white, with a high ruffled collar, long sleeves gathered at the wrists, and bib of smocked satin. This was the gown he'd removed last night in the heat of their lovemaking.

She stood mute, her head bowed, her black silky hair hiding her face, until he'd mastered the final button, which was embedded elusively in the lace and ribbons under her chin.

"Do your feet still hurt?"

"No." Her exhaled breath caught in a sob.

Gently he set her on the bed, pushed her back, and lifted her feet. "You'll be all right now." He tucked the blankets up around her neck, freeing her hair and arranging it carefully on the pillow. "Get some sleep. I'll bring you something to eat later."

"I won't want anything to eat. I'll only want to go home and never again lay eyes on you." She stared at the ceiling. "Everything is going around. You gave me too much whiskey."

"Close your eyes, Shel," he ordered in a voice laced with grief.

When she obeyed, tears spurted from under the black lashes. Before they wet the ribbons under her chin, she had passed out, a sad-angel expression caught on her face.

"Oh, my darling Shel . . ." There were no words to express what he was feeling. A pure unselfish surge of love swelled up from his chest and caught in his throat. Protectively, tenderly, he reached out and caressed a wing of her hair, then a cheek damaged by cold. "Darling sweet Shel . . . I nearly destroyed you. I don't blame you for hating me."

CHAPTER ELEVEN

She awoke to a mellow crimson light cast by the little bedside lamp. For a moment she was lost in a memory both wonderful and painful. Heath had drawn a chair to her bay window and sat looking out through the diamond-shaped panes, his dark profile brooding and contemplative.

Silent, she allowed her soft sad eyes to caress him. He was the only man she had ever wanted. Why was happiness always an elusive, ever-shifting chimera, never a tangible thing to be clasped and held to the breast lovingly, possessively? Why? Why?

"What time is it?"

Upon hearing her voice, he lowered his head. "About nine o'clock. You've been asleep several hours."

"Is the storm over?"

He laughed tonelessly at some inner joke, wagging his massive, shaggy head back and forth. "Yes, the storm is definitely over. How are you feeling?"

"Fine. A little headachy."

"That's from the whiskey."

"Probably," she agreed. Her senses were bewildered. Were people always so polite in the aftermath of tragedy?

Or had she and Heath fought each other until there was no fight left?

"I'll bring you some aspirin and something to eat." He shifted his booted feet clumsily and got wearily to his feet. "Do you need some help getting to the bathroom?"

"No," she assured him quickly. "I feel fine. Able to walk."

He averted his face and she wondered if he was embarrassed at having to be so concerned about her health and bodily functions.

"I'll be back in a little while with the food," he said gruffly.

She went to the bathroom, then brushed her teeth. Putting away the toothpaste, she looked in the cabinet mirror and was horrified by what she saw. Her once beautiful complexion was now red and mottled. It was as if the cold had seared it like scalding water.

She moaned softly and began to cry hurtful tears. Heath found her beside the bed sobbing into her hands. He lifted under her arms, turned her around, and held her close.

"I knew I shouldn't have left. Did you fall?"

"N-no, it's my face. Have you seen my face?"

He lifted her chin and tenderly caressed her hair. "Is that all? You'll heal in a few days."

"I'll never heal from all this. I'll never get over everything I've suffered."

He closed his eyes and seemed lost in darkness. She sensed his utter desolation. "You nearly died tonight, Shelby. I went crazy with fear. Fear is like a type of hell. It burns out the dross and purifies a man. And it makes a man want heaven more than anything else."

His large, capable hands fluffed her pillows, and he made her lie back. He straddled a bed tray over her and

181

pushed a strand of hair from her forehead. "Eat now," he ordered softly. "Grandfather made the soup especially for you. I brought you some tea and aspirin. Your headache will be gone soon, and the food will help you regain your strength."

Her chin wobbled and the food blurred before her eyes. She wanted to say something sarcastic, but his sweet tenderness was devastating.

He went back to the chair and sat down, leaving her alone. Obediently, she took up the tablets of aspirin, downed them with the tea, and then started on the soup. Amazing how one could still eat when the whole world lay in shards and fragments.

When she'd finished, he took the tray and set it on the dresser. Then he came back to sit beside her on the bed. He was wearing a strange, unstylish thermal pullover that made him look very unpretentious and homey. She resisted the impulse to reach out and touch him.

"We have to talk."

"I couldn't bear it," she begged tremulously. "Not after everything. The time for talking is over. It's too late."

His shoulders slumped as if under a heavy burden. "I need to know you, Shelby. I need desperately to know you."

"You didn't want to know me before."

"Don't accuse me, please."

"I refuse to tell you my heart, Heath. You must leave me something to take back home. Some shred of pride."

He left the bed and went to sit on the chair again. "Okay, if you won't talk then you can listen." He raked his hand through his hair and leaned forward, resting his elbows on his knees. "I fell in love with you seven years ago, Shelby. You were a gorgeous, blue-eyed, sexy girl who flattered me with adoring attention. I was scared of my feelings for you because I wanted to be free." He dropped his head and his voice became strained. "After that night in the motel room, I decided I had to get away from you to get you out of my blood. I was shocked to find out how old you really were, and guilt was added to my confused feelings. For several days I was crazy with indecision. Part of me wanted to wait for you to finish school and then get married. Another part urged me to deny everything and run."

She swiveled her head and her face took on an expression of incredulity. Still talking to his hands, he didn't see it.

"When Ralph touched you that night in the bar, something inside me snapped. It's a wonder I didn't kill him. God knows I wanted to."

"Sometimes you frighten me, Heath."

"Sometimes I frighten my own damn self. Grandfather says it will take a woman to tame me."

"You've had your women."

He laughed soundlessly. "My relationships have been very shallow and superficial. I've had nothing. This past year, until last night, I've barely touched a woman. That dinner date with Christine was an utter fiasco." He exhaled painfully. "I didn't tell anybody, but Grandfather somehow knew my feelings."

"You could have gotten your revenge long ago, you know. Your lawyer could have torn me apart on the stand."

"I couldn't let that happen. I was in love with you. It broke my heart when you wouldn't stand up for me at the trial. It just literally broke my heart. I told myself I hated you. And while I was in prison I began to believe it. I remembered the lies, and I agonized over the love affairs I knew you would be having."

"Oh, Heath," she cried softly. "If you only knew. I told you those lies so that you would pay attention to me. I didn't think you cared, and I wanted you to desperately." Once started, the words began to tumble out of her, haltingly at first and then with strength and determination. He had loved her; he had actually thought about marrying her. "I was determined to tell the world how I had pushed you to violence in that bar. You won't believe it." Her voice cracked. "I know you won't. But it was Father, Father and the damn precious Constantine name. His political career was rising and my stubborn determination to tell the truth would have been too damaging. He couldn't let his constituents know that his daughter had chased an older man, had seduced him, then driven him to violence. He persuaded, cajoled, and promised me the moon, but I would not give in. The prosecuting attorney was a personal friend of his, and they would get together and harass me. He assured me that you would be acquitted anyway and that my testimony, rather than helping you, would only damage my father. I half believed that. But still I stubbornly insisted on telling the truth."

"How did he finally get to you?" Heath asked quietly.

"Through Luann." Shelby sighed deeply.

He shook his head. "I don't get it."

"My father used emotional blackmail. He played on my sympathies and used my love for Luann against me. She was my only sister. She was the only one who really cared for me after Mother died."

"Then Luann talked you into remaining quiet at the trial?"

"No. She had no idea what Father was up to. She would

never have encouraged me to withhold the truth. She and Woody had only been married a year and she was pregnant with the twins. They lived with us because of their lack of finances, and Father made things pretty rough for them, especially Woody. Luann was afraid their marriage would break apart before it ever really got a chance. Woody got an opportunity to buy the grove property but couldn't swing it without my father's cosigning. Father agreed, giving them the chance finally to build a life of their own."

Heath pinched the skin between his brows and moaned softly. "And so Representative Constantine told you he would withdraw his financial support of your brother-in-law and sister unless you played along at the trial."

"Yes," she admitted in a small, wounded voice.

Heath gave a low, barely discernible curse.

She misunderstood his anger. "Oh, please believe me. I never meant to hurt you. Father promised me they would never send you to prison."

"I know," he said in tones meant to soothe her. "I guess I always knew there was more to it. Grandfather said you were not the type to deliberately set out to destroy a man. I should have listened to him and let you tell me this weeks ago. Besides, you weren't the one who got off a barstool and hit a man. Aaron was right in much of what he said this morning."

She relaxed against the pillow and searched the ceiling, her blue eyes glazed with the pain of remembering. "My nightmares about that court scene were awful. Sometimes I still have them. About a year after the trial, I had one while visiting Luann and Woody. It all came out. I thought Woody was going to go after Father and do something dreadful to him. He never could stand Father and still has a strong aversion to men like him—those who persecute and manipulate the weak and helpless."

Heath expelled a tremulous breath and covered his head with his hands. Still focused on the ceiling, Shelby didn't realize how her innocent comment had personally stabbed him.

"After that I went to live with Woody and Luann for a while. I helped her with the children, and Woody paid my way through secretarial school. He made a great success of the grove and managed to pay it off quickly, thereby severing Father's last hold on us. Father moved to Miami, became state representative, and married a news correspondent. I haven't seen him in three years. I haven't missed him, but I've missed having a father."

She drew the crimson comforter around her and wanted to cry. Heath remained silent, his hands still buried deeply in his hair.

"Luann . . ." She laughed, breaking her own morbid mood. "She's such a romantic idealist. Woody has protected her from so much. She can afford to believe in happy endings."

"Don't you believe in happy endings?" he asked, praying in the darkness of his soul.

She smoothed the coverlet. "No. I guess not."

He made an unintelligible sound.

"May I ask you another question?" he finally whispered.

"What is it?"

"How many men have there been besides me?"

She slithered into the depths of the bed. She couldn't tell him that. She just couldn't.

"How many?" he ordered relentlessly.

"None." Now he would know how much she had loved

him all these years. Now she had nothing left; she was totally humiliated. "I dated a lot of men, but I wouldn't let any of them touch me."

He hunched forward. "I suspected that last night. Not by anything you did . . . but by the way you made love to me. . . . Fresh and new . . . and virginal."

"Then why did you say all those terrible things to me this morning? Why did you ridicule what happened between us?"

"Because you wanted to leave me," he moaned. "I couldn't believe that after something so beautiful you wanted to leave me."

"I don't understand you at all," she wailed disconsolately. "What do you want of me? Why can't you just forgive me for the past? Why continue to probe at me and torture me? I liked you better when you were angry. At least then I could fight back. Say you've forgiven me, Heath. At least give me that much."

"Forgive you!" he exclaimed. "I should be the one asking that. I've nearly destroyed you. I took you away from the life you had made for yourself, forced you into an uninhabitable wilderness, then drove you out into a blizzard to die." He choked, his voice becoming cracked and hoarse. "Don't ask my forgiveness. Your crimes don't begin to compare with mine. At least yours were motivated by love. Love for me. Love for your sister."

His hands were shaking. She was struck dumb by his self-condemning speech. Before she could say anything, he burst out again.

"This whole mess is laughably ironic. Can't you see it? The captor has become the captive. My hate has turned into the deepest and most abiding love. I brought you here to break you, and here I am broken into a million pieces.

187

I ridiculed and tortured you. Now it's your turn. Forgiveness? No. I won't offend you by asking for it, although I'd get down on my knees if I thought it would do any good. After the things I've done . . . the things I've said . . ." A heartrending sob escaped from his throat before he could swallow it, and he broke down completely.

For a moment Shelby was too stunned to move. Finally she edged off the bed and walked over to kneel in front of him.

"Oh, don't," she breathed helplessly. Her hands fluttered to soothe his tear-ravaged face, to trace the fine lines beside his eyes and push back a lock of damp hair from his forehead.

Her lips comforted his trembling mouth, his fevered eyes, and the high cheekbones, now tasting of salt.

"This is killing me," he whispered. "I don't want your pity."

"I don't pity you." Her hands stroked his cinnamon-tinted hair, then moved down to his wide, tensely knotted shoulders. "I love you. I always have."

He swallowed thickly and lifted drugged hands to push her away. "You say that now, but tomorrow you will remember something I did to you. Something I said. You'll hate me again and want me to take you back to Florida."

She returned to kiss him and was pleased when he helplessly allowed it. "I'll get amnesia, Heath," she said. "We'll both get amnesia. The past will be forgotten. Right now can begin all our tomorrows. Oh, let's try," she cried brokenly. "Let's please try." She pressed her face against his, uniting their tears. "It can be beautiful."

He gathered her to him hungrily. "If you stay with me . . . I'll be so good to you, Shelby." His lips sought hers

blindly. "Don't leave me. . . . Don't ever leave me.
. . . I can't live without you."

He took her to the bed and worshiped her with his love,
his lips and tongue finding every curve, every sweet hol-
low, lingering, stopping to savor, then coming back to
draw sweetness from her lips again. Soon every inch of her
flesh had been intimately marked as his own personal
possession.

He was rough and tender, strong yet vulnerable, his love
words rolling over her again and again. Out of this all-
consuming fire, she assured him of her love, made promises. Her hands tried to catch him, pull at his clothes, but
he was constantly moving, giving, at times totally arrest-
ing her with a bold exploring mouth that gave her pleasure
so intense she cried out.

He leaned away long enough to take off his shirt, then
his pants. And when she saw him, she reached out, moaning softly, guiding him with insistent hands.

"Oh, Shell, I need you. I love you."

Their union was fierce and primitive, a perfect giving
and taking, a beautiful mingling of pantings and strangled
cries of rapture. They ascended higher and higher until a
splitting mutual ecstasy took them into a dark blue heaven
that may have lasted a moment or an eternity of eternities.

Sunshine woke them, intensely brilliant as it caught and
embraced the dazzling reflection of the snow. Shelby was
amazed. Montana weather was so unpredictable. Antarc-
tica one day; Sun Valley the next. Heath told her that they
were experiencing the well-known Montana chinook, a
strange warm breeze that came down from the mountains
at times and turned the snow to liquid diamonds.

They showered together in exciting and relaxing intima-
cy. Heath had become like a considerate husband. He

followed her with loving eyes and touched her often, as if to assure himself she was real and would not vanish.

The aroma of bacon, eggs, and coffee wafted around and through the woodwork to tantalize their nostrils. Joe Sam was flushing them out. Sheltered under the wing of Heath's arm, Shelby allowed him to escort her to the kitchen, wondering what Joe Sam would think. Surely the old sage knew that his grandson had spent the night in her room.

The table was beautifully set for two, complete with place mats and carefully folded cloth napkins. Shelby took her seat without looking Joe Sam's way. Heath greeted his grandfather, then fell on his food wolfishly, making some small talk about the winter feeding of the cattle.

Shelby looked up and found Joe Sam's shrewd eyes on her; she blushed all the way up to her hairline.

Joe Sam sat at the table while they ate, taking time over his pipe and a fresh cup of coffee. Shelby found his steamy scrambled eggs and crisp bacon delicious. Even the toast was the way she liked it—brown and crunchy and smeared with melted butter.

"And how are you feeling this morning?" Joe Sam finally addressed her directly. His black eyes were glittering with with something very like amusement. "Did you sleep well?"

"Yes, thank you."

"I thought so."

Yes, he was definitely teasing her. She shot him a warning look before concentrating on her marmalade and toast.

"Shelby and I are getting married, Grandfather."

Joe Sam puffed. "She'll make you a fine squaw." The corners of his mouth twitched humorously. "She'll give you many strong sons."

190

Shelby dropped the toast onto her plate and tried to stare him down. He merely continued to smoke innocently. After a perfectly timed pause, he added: "Nice, fine hips. Wide, like your grandma's. Excellent for birthing babies—Tanner babies."

Heath chuckled. "She's going to throw something at you in a minute, Grandfather." Impulsively, he took her chin between thumb and forefinger and made her look at him. "I love you, Summer Sky." Then he kissed her fully on the mouth right in front of Joe Sam. She broke away blushing. Heath laughed deeply, with sheer exuberant happiness.

Another laughter harmonized with his. Shelby looked up in surprise. Joe Sam's old stone face was split from ear to ear. Reaching toward him across the table, she began to laugh too. He clasped her hand with fatherly affection.

LOOK FOR NEXT MONTH'S
CANDLELIGHT ECSTASY ROMANCES ®